THE RED CROCODILE

WE THREE

STRUBEN CLINTON

0

Text © Struben Clinton
Illustrations © Jemima Catlin
Designed and printed by Ditto Press
Typeset in Caslon

First edition 2015
Published by Archaeopteryx Imprint
www.archaeopteryx-imprint.co.uk
ISBN 978-0993174759

We three had a secret we shared but spoke about with no one else. Not with our mothers and not with our brothers — well, Felix was too young anyway and Joe didn't care.

It began when I wrote to Roger Hein to remind him of that Easter when we were two very young boys. We met in a crazy Palace with fairy-tale turrets and a ski lift. We sat at the same table for breakfast, experimenting with the dozen sorts of cereal and jam, then we went out to ski and play at being spies chasing each other over the mountains.

So ten years later, when I was bored going to Dorset, with Grandfather and Joe painting all day and Mother being brave holding the twins' hands and paddling at the water's edge, I asked Roger if we could meet again for another skiing adventure. He wrote back yes, if I flew to Geneva he'd meet me and take me to stay with him in the Heinihof, their mountain chalet. His mother said we were old enough to look after ourselves, but not to make too much mess for the cleaner.

But then there was the problem of May.

May lived with her mother and step-father, Uncle Gus, in a pretty little villa in Kent, and our Grandfather's present home was the gatehouse at the end of their drive. Before he took up painting as a career, Grandfather had been in ship-building, mine-sweepers during the war and then yachts. Now he kept a small sail-boat off the Dorset coast where he had an old coastguard's cottage and when we went there in the holidays May came with him to go fishing. Mum liked having a girl along; at home she had a house full of us boys. However, when May heard I was flying to Geneva to go skiing she said she'd come with me instead. I wasn't at all keen to have her along, spoiling my fun with Roger.

But one can't say no to May.

When I met Roger ten years ago I'd been terribly jealous of his bushy mop-head of emphatic red while I had childishly spiky straw for hair — now mercifully toned down to a nondescript dark blond — but when Roger and May met they laughed at each other, seeing they both had really red hair:

Roger's now trimmed to a tufty short chestnut in contrast to May's wildly goldy-copper, the difference probably influenced by Roger's fierce old Jewish grandfather's gingery-grey beard and May's weirdish Irish mother, the Divine Sibyl.

"This is the *Heinihofli*," said Roger when we arrived at the chalet.

May and I were united in mirth when we saw it, so slopey-roofed big, its balconies of freshly planted out geraniums bedecked with red and white checked tea-towels against the night-frost.

"I know it's somewhat incongruous," said Roger. "It's considered less ostentatious to be in the vernacular but it's really a bit of a a joke as if wealth is counted in a million petals of the right red. Pink is vulgar. We have a gardener for the window boxes."

Inside under the high peak of the roof was a huge open space with table-tennis and billiards around a circle of glowing coals that burst into little flames at the turn of a knob in the middle. We liked it a lot and in the evening we took a pot of chunky pea soup with sausage and a pile of cheese sandwiches up there for our supper. We didn't go near Mrs Hein's sitting room, dedicated to her exquisite flower paintings — "completely out of cha-racter," said Roger, "and if Dadi Hein had his way he wouldn't have a chalet, he'd have built an elegant concrete tower instead, with a helipad on the roof."

As it was, they had a short landing strip in a fairly flat field.

"It's never used now," said Roger. "I'll be getting a Porsche next year for my birthday. It's a bribe so I'll stay at home and learn on the shop-floor. I'd rather go to Zürich and get a degree in engineering first."

"You're lucky," said May. "I'd leave school at once if I had a factory to go and work in."

"You're too young," said Roger.

"No I'm not," said May, "my Daddy said I could work with him in the place with the bears only he went away and didn't come back. I'm really annoyed with him."

May had her worst grouchy face on but then she suddenly looked cheerful again so I knew she had thought of something to do about it. I dreaded to think what.

"My step-father Gus is nice but useless," she said. "He's a Doctor of Philosophy and spends all week in Lincoln's Inn arguing with crooks and criminals — not the ordinary kind who mug people for petty cash but the clever ones. He loves it, especially when he gets a really tricky case. He says my Daddy was the trickiest of all, he's sorry too that he went away. He misses him."

"Your Daddy!" I said, getting impatient with her. "And what about mine? Mine was the best Dad in the world only Mum says it was a big mistake that he sold his factory so all he had was a hideous great heap of loose money rattling around instead of tied up in neat Swiss bundles, and with no proper work to go to every day he went wandering around the world looking for trouble. That's what got him in the end."

"Your doting mother has the silliest ideas about what money is," said May.

I knew May was right but I liked Mum's way of thinking that made sense of it to her.

"She says she's happy that he left her with a nice smooth river of cash that flows along quietly and all she has to do is phone the bank manager when she needs any and he sends a polite young woman around with some in a briefcase. Her job is to count it out slowly so Mum knows exactly what she has, and add it to whatever is left over in the safe from the last time. Sometimes he comes himself just to have a talk and discuss school fees and that kind of thing and whether or not she should give more to *Guide-dogs for the Blind* or the *Lifeboats*."

It seemed the clashing red-heads brought out the worst in both of them. Roger, though he had been skiing all his life, had the Swiss anxiety thing of always needing to do better in spite of already being the best, while May, though tobogganing down the drive in Kent was her only experience of snow, had no doubts about her ability to ski the best. She upset Roger with her competitiveness. I was pig in the middle and had to be the peace-keeper, as usual. My Uncle Paul says it's our destiny, his and mine that is, and to be proud of it. But, I thought, diplomacy is his choice of career; I didn't want to spend the rest of my life settling other people's quarrels. My mother says Uncle Paul is my proper rôle model. She doesn't like the Swiss, she says it's impossible to be friends with them though she wouldn't interfere with me. She trusts me.

"Remember Smiley?" said Roger. "I liked him the best."

"Smiley is the one who took us skiing and told us all about war and how to fight in the mountains," I told May. "Only I was really too young then, maybe Roger remembers better."

"Of course I do," said Roger. "I was ten, you were only six. You weren't bad though for a little boy. Smiley was the greatest fun."

"I loved him too," I said, feeling what was missing about this holiday, but Roger caught me up on it and said:

"Come on, we'll go and find the place where he said he'd push you over the edge if you couldn't keep your skis straight and stop falling with your nose in the snow. It'll cheer May up to know how bad you were."

"As long as you don't gang up on me," I said.

Growing up in a large family I often felt the odd one out. It wasn't as if May were my real friend, she was just someone I'd known all my life, nevertheless I'd feel bad if she became better chums with Roger than with me. This business of growing up was tiresome. It was easier when we used to fight and then fall asleep together in the May's bed. May's room was mine too when I stayed in the Divine Sibyl's *casino* in Kent. But not in London at Mum's. May's place there was in Mum's dressing room so she could be a surrogate daughter.

I begrudged May getting Roger too, he started out as my friend, not hers.

Roger kitted us out with *Langlauf* skis and we set off to find traces of Smiley in the snow of ten years ago. I couldn't recognise anything, one snowfield is much the same as another, but Roger knew where he was going as he zigzagged back and forth, leaving May and me to plod along in a more or less direct line, catching up with him when he swooped across us in the middle of a zig or a zag. He reminded me of Smiley the way he scouted around. This was reassuring.

When I saw the pointed spire and the turret of the Palace on a hill in the distance I knew we were re-entering familiar territory.

"Here it is," Roger called out, "this is where you didn't fall into the abyss."

A rocky slope with tops of the trees down below us — even now I wouldn't want to go skidding down there. It would be hard to climb back up.

"If you were injured down there you'd just freeze to death," said Roger. "People do in Switzerland, every year at least a dozen."

But not me, not as long as I had Smiley's Roger to rely on.

May was busy practicing up and down the slope. She stopped when she heard the hum and clack of an electric train in the distance. The little town was down there below the Palace and May wanted to know where the trains went to. She liked plotting and planning, organising and solving problems. At home she had a younger sister and two brothers so that gave her plenty of scope.

In our house it was more a situation of Joe and me working together to squash the sacred twins Axie and Boris when they got too uppity. They were like that because when they were born Dad had brought a small brown woman called Wilhelmina home with him from Djakarta to look after them. She was supposed to be a mid-wife but really she was a goona-goona witch and spent her time ruining the hygiene of our boring stainless steel kitchen with her magic brews. Joe and I loved her and she made marvellous food for us. Mum never went near the kitchen so she didn't know what was going on except that she complained about the funny smells when she was having her breakfast of yoghurt and banana in her morning-room. while the twins perched on their stools in the kitchen and let the witch feed them a soupy nutty mess. But now that they were twelve they couldn't go on relying on magic to get by in life. Our mother and the aunts all adored them, they had only Joe and me to teach them sense.

Roger never had anyone to boss until May and I came along.

"Do you think Smiley would have really pushed you over the edge?" he asked me now, as if I should know the answer.

"Remember he told us he had fallen down a ravine and how he managed to climb out," I reminded him.

"I never knew if he were joking or not," Roger admitted.

"When I fell he never helped me up, he always just said 'Try harder!'"

"Or 'fall better!'" said Roger.

"He probably thought we should be prepared to climb out of trouble like he always did."

"I was thrilled to be allowed go out with someone so tough," said Roger, "that's what made him exciting — though I was surprised that my mother, who had known him really well for a long time, sent me off into the mountains with only him to take care of me. I used to say to him that she'd be cross if I got hurt. 'Yes,' he said, 'she'd think it very stupid of you. You'll never be boss of a spy-ring if you can't keep your wits about you.' So we'd take turns hiding and tracking."

"You never let me do any hiding," I said.

"You were too small to be let loose alone, if we couldn't find you soon enough, you might really have frozen. You were the kind of obstinate little bugger who would sit tight to the bitter end."

Roger and I started to make boy jokes about "girls" because May would never stick to a plan, she'd go wandering off to amuse herself. We got so used to it that when she did disappear we didn't even notice she was gone until dinner time. It wasn't likely she wouldn't be on time for her dinner. Roger had a cupboard full of ready-made rösti, eggs and bacon, cheese, apples and muesli, and a mountain of chocolate bars, so we didn't need to go shopping. But May had been asking about buying sandwiches and Roger told her the Migros supermarket was best, so we decided to go and ask about her there before raising an alarm to get the mountain rescue team out. A tall red-haired English girl in a bright red anorak was conspicuous enough to be noticed, and sure enough we were told she had been in quite early and was seen walking down the street opposite towards the station.

At the station she had bought a monthly rail pass so they couldn't say what her destination might be.

Well, obviously she wasn't lost in the snow.

"Or kidnapped," I said.

"People don't get kidnapped in Switzerland," said Roger. "It's not done."

So we went back to the chalet and ate our dinner.

"I hope she comes back before I have to tell the Divine Sibyl that we've lost her," I said.

"If she's really a Sibyl she'll know where to find her," said Roger.

He was right, of course, but we didn't know that then. It seemed too far-fetched.

"Maybe she wants to see if we are really spy-catchers," I said.

"All right," said Roger, " if she isn't back by morning we'll go hunting a silly girl spy."

We stood on the platform and it was the toss of a coin in which direction we began our search. The first train that came in happened to be for Montreux. If she'd decided to fly home she'd have to change trains in Montreux, so someone might have seen her there.

"But that's actually the least likely," I said. "She'd never just go home."

"So we'll go the other way," said Roger.

When we got down to the junction at Spiez the choice was between east, west & up. We thought she might have headed up where the highest mountains were but if she had done that yesterday where would she have spent the night? Up on the Jungfraujoch or maybe Grindelwald for the view? She could have found a hut to shelter in for the night. But we were a day late so we'd have to think a day ahead to catch up.

"She might have dawdled a while in Kleine Scheidegg to see if any rock-climbers were falling to their death off the North Face, but knowing May, not for long."

"This is no good," said Roger. "If we were spy-catchers we'd have a plot to follow. But a fifteen-year-old girl? Who can guess what's in her head? "

"She's probably at the *Heinihof* eating sausages wondering where we've gone," I said.

"We'd better phone your Divine Sibyl for advice."

Much as I dreaded telling the Sibyl we'd lost her daughter, as usual she had the answer almost before I posed the question.

"May took a train somewhere and we don't know where she is," I said.

"Probably her father's office in Bern. He promised she could go and work there when she is old enough so maybe she has decided the time has come. Maybe she'll even find him there."

She was mocking herself for entertaining a forlorn hope.

I remembered him as a presence, as elusive as a smell, oak-moss, bergamot. May might well encounter him that way, lingering as a ghost in one of his favourite haunts.

Taking a train to Bern was the easy part, but what then?

Sit on a terrace and wait for her to pass by, was Roger's proposal.

"In Bern everyone does, sooner or later," he said.

He was right. In Bern then no one was in a hurry and eventually we spotted her sauntering down the middle of the street as if she owned it, as laconique about the trolleybuses as a bull-runner in Pamplona. We followed her, keeping our distance, weaving through the busy arcades until she turned into a cross alley of dark heavy arches where she disappeared from view. The only place she could have gone was up some steps and through a door beside which hung a lighted board with a list of names.

"Let's guess," said Roger, delighted with our spy-catching success so far.

On the first floor was a doctor, specialist in nervous disorders; the embassy of a small South American country on the 2nd; a private bank on the 3rd; Medical Technik on the 4th and *Totenkopf (Schweiz) GmbH* on the 5th.

"Medical instruments were my Dad's specialty," I said, "but it's the wrong name."

"I'd bet on *Totenkopf*," said Roger.

We walked up the stairs checking on each landing for likely signs of May but any of the doors that were open revealed daunting Swiss receptionists the sight of whom repelled us.

Until 5.

There we were received by a small hunchback man of indeterminate age sitting at a desk with a phone and a ledger.

His subsequent conversation with Roger in drawly Bernese was incomprehensible to me. Roger condensed it for me into: he wants to know if we have business for Totenkopf. I asked what kind of business and he says if we don't know, the answer is no and go away.

"We're looking for a girl called May," I said, getting impatient with this Swiss chattery beating about the bush.

"The answer is still no," he said, or words to that effect.

When Roger made a move towards the inner door the little man whipped a gun out of a drawer and pointed towards the exit.

"We'll come back with the police," said Roger.

"Just try," said Mini-man.

We went and sat on the stairs outside to consider our next move.

"This is silly," I said. "She's in there for sure. He can't actually shoot us."

"People often get shot in Switzerland," said Roger.

It really was an up-side-down country: no to kidnapping but yes to shooting, apparently.

"May could have decided to stay here," said Roger, "so she may possibly not come out again today. We can't sit here all night."

"What would Smiley do?" I asked.

"He'd have a gun and shoot first," said Roger.

"But if the little man is a friend of May's I wouldn't want to hurt him," I said.

Luckily May herself came out of the *Totenkopf (Schweiz) GmbH* door and sat down on the steps beside us.

"What are you doing here?" she asked.

"That's what we want to know."

"I'm just going about my business. You boys can go back to playing games."

"We can't leave you here alone…"

"I'm not alone, I'm with Grimsi…"

"Who on earth is Grimsi? he looks quite sinister."

"Yes, he makes the most of it. Sometimes genuinely sinister people come in."

"But what are you doing?"

"Our business. My Daddy told me what I had to do before he went away and Grimsi was expecting me to turn up. So good-bye. I'll come and see you on Saturday."

When we got back to the *Heinihof* I phoned the Divine Sibyl to say she was right: May had taken over her father's office in league with a troll called Grimsi.

"Don't expect me to do anything about her," I added quickly before she could ask for the impossible.

"No need, dearest Conrad," Divine Sibyl said. "It's a job for mothers."

But it wasn't Mother Sibyl who came but Roger's, Mrs Hein. She arrived at the *Heinihof* on Friday evening driving her yellow Diablo. She kissed me on both cheeks and said: "So you are the Angel's boy!"

She looked me up and down critically. I couldn't guess what kind of judgement she was making but it was disconcerting; I was used to the unreserved approval of all mothers.

"Heini chartered a Fokker to take the whole Swiss-load over to London for your parents' wedding," she said. "It was a splendid occasion but we knew it couldn't last — she was far too good for him."

I was speechless. Everyone knew my Mum and Dad adored each other, I knew it myself from being a child with their extravagant love all around me. It lasted until Dad went to Buenos Aires to play polo and drowned crossing the River Plate. Not the kind of end to it Mrs Hein seemed to suggest. I decided on the spot not to confide in her anything about May.

Mrs Hein had brought a roast chicken for our supper which made a nice change from sausages. She tried to talk to me about School and what exams I was taking and that kind of rubbish but I was too offended to talk to her.

"Just like your father," she said. A thin, dark-haired woman with a sharp face, I felt she was laughing at me.

It was only when she showed curiosity about our oddity twins that I forgot and told her the funny stories about them. I didn't mention goona-goona but told how they swopped names, Axie for Boris and Boris for Axie, to keep us confused so one never knew who had done what, how they told lies about Joe and me and made up stories to try and get us to do things for them. They went and sang songs for our very ancient uncle monk Harold. He was a bit ga-ga and believed they were genuine angels and had them stay at the monastery to talk about heaven, and teach him new hymns for the chapel of the Holy Innocents. Our Mum stopped them being too silly at home but she was no match for a band of crazy old monks encouraging their daftness. They loved our mother but the one they respected was the DivineSibyl; her magic was as good as theirs and they paid attention to what she said. Joe and I wished she'd adopt them and maybe let us have Felix instead. Felix was May's younger brother and a terrific little fellow. He could play games without cheating or crying. We knew we'd never get Willie, he belonged to Uncle Gus and Gus's fearsome old Father William. It seemed to me families don't always get the right children — even Roger. How did über-cool Roger end up belonging to über-Swiss Mami and Dadi Hein?

May walked in on Saturday morning while I was moodily picking hazel-nuts out of the muesli. Mrs Hein had taken Roger in the yellow Diablo down to shop for something to eat more interesting than sausage and rösti and left-over chicken.

"I don't like Mrs Hein," I told May. "Roger says she was very fond of Smiley but she was very rude about my Dad."

May didn't care about that, she hated my Dad — she said he smelt of sweet tonka bean that's deceptively fragrant mixed with wickedly earthy truffles — and she had never met Smiley. So I asked her to tell me about Grimsi.

"I'm really happy that I found him," she said. "My Daddy left him in charge of the office when he went away and Grimsi kept the business ticking over, mainly for the sake of a couple of big clients in Africa and an art and antiques dealer in Basel called Mr Mug. Now I'm here we can expand and get it going properly again."

It occurred to me to question the legality of the *GmbH* in the company name but there were so many unknown factors that it was better to say nothing. May certainly had no doubt about her right to take over and carry on as if nothing had happened to the legal owner of the name.

"You can't leave school yet, you'll have to go back," I pointed out rather feebly as my only protest.

"I can go to any old Swiss school for a few months until I'm sixteen," she said, "just to learn to speak properly, and Grimsi will find someone useful to take me on for a couple of years training — I'd like to do aircraft, I can get to the works by train, Grimsi says everyone does in Switzerland..."

May went on nattering about planes and flying and other pie in the sky. That made me think about my Dad's lovely big office-study at home, really the most important room in the house with tall arched windows and a wide balcony over the street and the greenery of the square opposite. It was just as he had left it, now unused. Uncle Paul had suggested he could use it as a constituency office but Mum wouldn't let him upset it with party politics so he gave that idea up. But if May could just walk into her father's office in Bern and the mysterious Grimsi business, so could I at home. Joe had Grand-father's old studio off the garden for painting in, so Dad's study was really all mine. Only I'd have to find out what exactly he did there or think of some-thing worthwhile for myself.

"What kind of business do you and Grimsi do?" I asked. "I can't see how Mr Mug's art and antiques come into your *Totenkopf (Schweiz) GmbH*."

"Weapons and musical instruments — but that has nothing to do with you," May answered.

"I don't want anything to do with it," I snapped back.

To demonstrate that I too could undertake a serious project I'd get Uncle Paul with his diplomatic pass to come with me to South America and bring Dad's body back. If he were buried in Highgate across the Heath from where he'd been born, Mum would have a proper grave to visit, then she'd have to stop thinking he might still some day come home. I could understand that Uncle Paul hadn't done that sooner, the fighting and political turmoil would have made it difficult. The war was over though it might be a bit tricky still with the Argies in a bad mood, but together we could surely do it.

I felt happy that I had something that gave me a focus to think about ins-tead of boring old A-level Latin and Greek, French and German, languages I had chosen because it wasn't really a choice at all, language is what one does all day anyway.

Mrs Hein and Roger came back just as May was fidgeting about being hungry and poking around in the kitchen and picking at my pile of hazelnuts.

"My Goodness!" said Mrs Hein, "Another! Whose is this one?"

"May belongs to the Divine Sibyl and Uncle Gus," I put in quickly to stop May blabbing her usual nonsense.

"The red hair seems to be infectious," Mrs Hein said, unpacking the bags of food on the table. May took a fresh croissant.

"We're the remnants of the Celtic fringe," she said, munching hungrily, shedding flakey crumbs, "clinging on at the edges of Europe's crumbling landmass. My Daddy says that by the time they've wiped us out down to the last man, the whole world will be Chinese."

Whatever about the Celts, May certainly had a banshee of a mother.

"It'll be left to us in the western isles," said May "to fight them off, and a few Helvetii lurking above the Alpine passes chucking rocks at passing strangers," she added, looking at Roger the Magnificent Rock-Chucker. May, like her Daddy before her, liked imagining doom scenarios.

"Not me," said Roger. "I'm a city boy, hurling rocks by way of sport and yodelling is not my idea of fun."

"You're an anomaly," said Roger's mother, "A random gene that cropped up out of nowhere."

I looked at him with a critical eye. Then leaned over and whispered behind his mother's back:

"Maybe a random Smiley gene."

Roger shook his head at me which I took as a warning to shut up.

May studied Mrs Hein from head to foot instructing Roger in not over-cooking the veal cutlets. When we sat down to eat she said: "Will you take me shopping, Mrs Hein? I need townie clothes."

"Of course, I'd be delighted," said Mrs Hein and looked genuinely pleased.

So May joined Mrs Hein in the yellow Diablo and they drove off together so May could study how to be a sophisticated business woman — whatever the business was that she conducted with her Grimsi and wouldn't let me in on — certainly not art and antiques.

I phoned the Divine to tell her the latest development.

"Oh, dear," she said, "not the dreaded Mrs Hein! I'll be lucky if I ever get my daughter back. But Mrs Hein is certainly an expert in buying clothes."

It was a great relief that May was safely out of the way so Roger and I could go trekking cross-country without her to worry and distract us, until the holiday was over and I had to go back for School.

"If you come again in the summer," Roger said, "we can go for a really long cross-country hike and stay in Alpine Club huts on the way — Switzerland is a land one can satisfactorily criss-cross with a sense of achievement without being a pilgrim to Rome or having to go all the way to Compostela."

I was gratified that he wanted me to come with him, it was as good as having an older brother. So I asked him again about Smiley.

"I knew him because he was a friend of my parents," said Roger, a bit stiffly I thought. "He was my father's adjutant in the army. Swiss men usually make their friends in the army — he started work as an apprentice in the Heini workshop..." then he stopped, dissatisfied with his explanation. "Dadi Hein is a good father, but I used to imagine how marvellous it would be if I had Smiley instead. He seemed more genuine somehow, kind of like me. Dadi Hein can be very irritating at times."

Just as I thought.

"Not that it matters now," he added regretfully.

16

Smiley was gone, like the others, no one knew when or where. Spies just go and don't come back. It made me all the more determined to fetch Dad's body home. Now the idea was in my head, I hated it that he had been left there unloved half-way around the world.

May was booked on the same flight home as I, so I asked Roger to phone his mother to find out where she was. Mrs Hein reported that May had bought herself what she considered suitable clothes — not quite what Mrs Hein would have chosen — and had gone on her way, she didn't know where.

"That girl is so like her father it's scary," she said. The charm of having a daughter to go shopping with had rapidly worn off — just as Mum got nowhere with girl-talk either. Only the Divine Sibyl could deal with a daughter like May.

"We'd better go to the airport via Bern to see if we can tear her away from the Grimsi troll," I said.

I had no doubt that that's where she would be. We'd kidnap her if necessary.

"I told you — one doesn't kidnap people in Switzerland," said Roger. "It's not done."

"I will if I can," I said, quoting my Dad.

"That's what Smiley said too," said Roger, "but the fact is that you can't. Grimsi would shoot us."

"We'll wait outside and hustle her into the car when she comes out."

"We can't get a car into the Lauben," Roger pointed out "and we certainly can't drag her screaming out to the street. That wouldn't be acceptable. Someone would feel obliged to call the police."

"All right, what would Smiley do?"

"Damn all. He'd leave her to go to hell in her own good time."

Needless to say, I flew to London without May.

When I got home I crept through the area door into the basement and managed to get half-way up to my room without meeting anyone on the way.

On the landing outside Dad's study I hesitated, then turned the doorknob. I couldn't remember when I'd last been here, probably when Mum and Uncle Paul were discussing it, and now I looked in with trepidation, almost expecting ghosts. The silence was heart-breaking. The most eerie thing was that there was a tiny green light blinking on the long table among the array of telephones and other devises. A single tiny sign of life, a signal from some distant star perhaps. The machines were active even if Dad wasn't, Grimsies keeping his disembodied spirit alive.

I went on up past Mum's room and the twins' to the floor above where mine was and Joe's bedroom, though Joe seldom came up now he had the studio. Joe and I had the front of the house, and at the back overlooking the garden was Uncle Paul and Aunt Madge's sitting-room that used to be our wonderland play-room when we were little. I knocked on their door and looked in.

Paul was watching the international news via the satellite dish he'd had installed on a post in the garden. They were talking about the economic situation in the newly independent Soviet states since the end of the cold war.

"They want me to set up a new consulate..."

"Please don't go to Russia," I said, alarmed that we were going to lose him too.

"Don't worry," he said. "I can get out of it. It's not a job I fancy."

"I want to go and get Dad. It's time we brought him back."

Paul switched off the television, stood up and went to one of the windows looking out into the trees of ours and adjoining London gardens.

"Where is he buried?" I asked, puzzled by this hesitation.

"We don't know," he answered.

"Don't know? Why... How...?"

"Well, as your father was a Swiss national..."

Was he? Did I know this? I was suddenly unsure of what I did know, what I thought I knew.

"When he was reported dead they would have been obliged to repatriate the body, but they couldn't find it. The Argentine authorities denied that they knew of any such person. The only credible witness was a woman from Buenos Aires who said they had wanted to question him about some people he was seen talking to so she had taken him to hide out in her holiday cabin on the coast in Uruguay and it was there it happened."

"But you told us he was drowned in the river crossing over on the ferry."

"Well, the various accounts were conflicting. A body wearing his distinctive crocodile leather coat was fished out of the river but when the Swiss looked into it, it wasn't him. Then this woman said it wasn't the River Plate but the Solis Chico, a small river much further east. They sent a representative to find out, but there no one would say if they knew anything about him. The trouble was of course that at that time people were too frightened to talk, innumerable bodies were being dumped in the sea, so it was impossible to get to the truth. But there was no doubt about the sincerity of the woman because she was taking a great risk in approaching a foreign bank official at all. She said she hoped he would inform the consul because she felt she owed it to her *amigo* as he had been very good to her, generous and kind. We assume he gave her real money — American dollars. That they were lovers the Swiss could only surmise."

I listened with growing dismay. All my certainties were undone.

"Now you have raised the question yourself, you are old enough to know the real situation. Your mother's loss is grief enough, I can't make it worse by saying there is any doubt about what happened or ambiguity about bodies."

"But it's different now," I said. "We could ask questions now and get answers."

"In Uruguay possibly, in Buenos Aires that's not so sure. Telling the truth has never been their strong point. Give it another year, when you are eighteen you'll be better able to deal with all that."

I had relied on my Uncle Paul too long, now I had to grow up fast. I wished I had Roger to talk it over with, or even May. It was no use talking to either Grandfather or Joe. They were concentrating on Joe getting a portfolio together for entrance to St Martins or Camberwell. They both avoided any emotional disturbance at the best of times and now certainly didn't want to be bothered with anything that distracted them from Art, as if that were the only thing worthwhile — though there could hardly be a more import-ant subject than the fate of one's father, in art or anywhere else.

I went to find Mum in her cosy little sitting-room — as opposed to the cool elegance of her drawing-room — and told her that instead of going back to School to finish working for A-levels I wanted to do the International Baccalaureate in Geneva. I knew she wouldn't object. She had gone to a quaintly old-fashioned girls' academy in Geneva herself when she was about my age, in 1970. I was quite right, she took to the idea with enthusiasm saying it would be an advantage for if I followed her brother into the diplomatic service. That wasn't my intention but I didn't say so. All I wanted was to share my life with Roger and May. It would be easy to get from Geneva to the Grimsi burrow or the Heinihof up in the Bernese Oberland, and when Roger had the promised Porsche he would enjoy zooming down to see me. I did feel a certain regret about leaving my chums at School but that all seemed pointless now I had a definite plan to work towards.

"And may I add the new Macintosh computer to the array on Dad's desk? He'd want it kept up-to-date."

"Yes," she said. "He trusted you, he wouldn't mind you using his machines. Oh, dear Con, how well you two used to get on! He was such a marvellous father, especially for you, the eldest. He was so happy when you were born, to have a lovely little boy of his own! He used to say he had such a happy childhood, he wanted you to have the same."

"And you're a lovely mother," I said and hugged her.

Dad used to hug her and say the same.

"And these unholy twins are damned lucky to have you too," I concluded as they came in, hiding their cherub faces under the hideous peaky base-ball caps Mum's American friend had brought them. I'd be glad to have left School before they started next September. Joe too, though School had a perfectly good art department, wouldn't have to be big brother to the awful twins.

Joe was down in Kent with Grandfather. Grandfather was really a naval architect — mine-sweepers had been the highlight of his career — but now his portraits earned him quite a lot of money, to his surprise, and in between painting he cultivated Kentish wild-flower meadows on Uncle Gus's land and did bee-keeping instead of fishing off the Dorset coast.

Joe enjoyed staying in the gatehouse where the twins couldn't annoy him or the Sibylline children who had always filled him with dread, but now the summer half would begin soon so it was time for me to go down to help him bring his paintings and gear home. He would probably have to wait until September before he could escape School, but I told Grandfather my plan was to go and enjoy the jolly boating weather on the lake in Geneva instead.

"Ever on and up," said Grandfather with the usual sarcastic tolerance with which he dealt with his numerous grandchildren. "From Seahouses village school to Durham grammar to posh public school and now up into the rarefied heights of international scholarship. Not bad going for a few short generations of Vikings."

"For my admission I have to write them an essay about myself and my goals in life. I don't know if I should say that my only goal at the moment is to go and find my Dad's body to bring it home. Or should I keep quiet about that and say something less emotive?"

"Is that what you're really going to do?" asked Joe. "Can I come with you?"

"That is not exactly a career choice," said Grandfather.

"I can't think about a career until I done that," I said. I didn't want to mention the array of winking lights beckoning me, besides I couldn't understand why he seemed so indifferent to what had happened to his only son. "It's a kind of destiny thing."

"You'd better consult the Sibyl," said Grandfather.

So I did.

But first I had to tell her about May. She was taking it surprisingly well.

"I knew she would sooner or later," she said. "May has been heading that way since she was four when her father gave her her little red passport and showed her where she could go to work — at the time her only ambition was to earn enough money to buy a bulldog like Madge's. I didn't know there was a Grimsi involved but that's reassuring somehow, maybe he'll do instead of the bulldog."

The Divine Sibyl was the name the family gave her, half as a joke but also because men were in awe of her and her quite extraordinary power over them. I loved her because she had taken care of me as a baby and she loved me as if I were her own child. She was best friends with my Mum though they didn't do things together, Mum had a different kind of friends for shopping and playing golf.

Of course, we knew that the Sibyl and my Dad had had a long if sporadic love affair. I used to spy on them and had seen how on fire he was and how much pleasure he gave her. It gave me the feeling that I was in love with her too. Anyone else's bum was rude but hers was creamy pink and gorgeous. Mum didn't hold it against her, in fact it seemed to give them a friendship based on mutual understanding and trust. Now that he was gone they had each other to talk to about him, though it was mostly Mum who talked, perhaps to maintain her legal possession in the face of the Sibylline enchantment, while the Sibyl gazed cryptically into the distance, I suppose seeing visions. Would I ever have two such splendid women so in love with me?

Dad had had a penthouse apartment overlooking the Thames where he used to go when he wanted to get away from everyone to have a quiet time with his music. After he had been gone seven years Uncle Toby, who acted for him as his solicitor, sold the apartment for a lot of money which he divided half to Mum and half spread out amongst us children. Joe and I got our own bank accounts straight away, though not the twins, they'd only do something crazy like running away from home. But it was the Divine Sibyl who got the musical instruments. That included his grandmother's Steinway piano and a nice violin, so her share was not insignificant. Mum didn't begrudge her having the Steinway as centre-point in the casino's octagonal hall, it seemed a better place for it rather than have it clutter up Mum's drawing-room, and the Sibyl actually played romantic sad sonatas on it.

As for the violin, Mum hardly knew it existed. I noticed it when I went to visit the *casino* as it was in a glass case in Uncle Gus's Archive under the one and only portrait of Dad, what he called his *memento mori* — Grandfather promised Mum he'd paint a drawing-room one for her but somehow he couldn't get around to doing it. When I was old enough to take an interest, a violin with the same name, a *Guernari del Jesú,* made headlines in the Sunday papers being sold to a collector in Oregon for a staggeringly huge sum. When I asked the Divine if she realised how much the violin was worth she said:

"Yes, that's why I have it. Your Dad knew I wouldn't sell it but cherish it for him for always. Now Felix shows promise to play as well or better than your Dad did, if he ever plays really well enough he can use it. An instrument ought to be played, not kept in a bank vault for the sake of the number of noughts on its price tag."

So the Sibyl should be glad that I was going to bring him home again.

But she wasn't.

"You won't find him," she said.

"But Paul knows all about what happened," I protested. "We'll go together."

But she only shook her head and wouldn't say any more.

"Wretched woman," said Grandfather when I told him. "She sees ghosts. So don't expect any practical advice from her, you know how misleadingly ambiguous the Sibyl is."

More than ever I needed May. And Roger. So I completed my application, paid the fees and set off into the future.

I didn't expect to like the Swiss school, but I didn't care much as long as I got through the next two years. However, it was much better than I anticipated. I appreciated what a privilege it had been to get the best education available in England, but now what I was learning seemed more relevant to my real life. What was discussed in my class of bright internationals, amongst whom I could easily hold my own, seemed more relevant to my big adventure.

When I tried to phone May at *Totenkopf (Schweiz) GmbH* I was answered by Grimsi who denied all knowledge of her. Nevertheless, not long after May phoned me.

"What do you want?" she asked.

"To tell you I'm in Geneva now and can we meet? I have stuff I want to talk over with you."

When May saw my school she decided it would suit her better than the one she was attending in Bern. Goodness knows what rigmarole she told the admissions office to persuade them to let her in, she told me they said yes to her simply because she was exactly the kind of pupil they liked.

"Did you tell them about Grimsi?" I asked.

"Of course. Grimsi clinched it."

I didn't believe her. But it was exciting to have May around talking nonsense again.

"I can start as soon as my money clears. As I have a Swiss bank it shouldn't take long."

"Is that Totenkopf money?" I asked, curious what source of supply she had. The Sibyl didn't have a lot of money to give her a huge allowance, and Uncle Gus was too prudent.

"Yes. I pay myself a director's salary."

"Who decides how much?"

"I do. I'm taking a course in business management. Even though Grimsi knows everything, it's as well to have a second opinion. And aerodynamics. I said I wanted to be an apprentice in the aircraft factory but they said I was too young for such a macho *environ* — lucky my French is good, thanks to jolly Miss Butler — but I can do theory for a few years until I'm *klug* enough to deal with the *garçons*. Actually I am already, I'm tall and strong and I've got you and two brothers but I'll go along with what they say for now. I'll take flying lessons as soon as they'll let me. My Daddy warned me it's tiresome being a genius in a world of mere mortals."

"Dad said character is what counts: courage, integrity and common sense," I said.

"Your Dad? Well he knew there was no point in talking to you about being a genius, thickhead."

"I'm going to Buenos Aires to get his body and bring it home."

"You won't find it," May said, just like her mother, but May was no prophetess so I didn't need to pay much attention to her.

"What would you know about it?" I said.

"That it's common sense," she said. "After years of sheer hell with thousands of dead, how are you going to dig them all up and identify the right one? There may well be more than one skull with red hair attached."

"He was six foot one and had one slightly crooked tooth," I said, nevertheless somewhat daunted by her description of the task. "Besides Uncle Paul said there was a woman witness who can point out where it happened."

"Well good luck in finding her! You'd do better consulting Mama. She's marvellous at finding things. She just closes her eyes and thinks, and then tells you where to look. She just knows. She says it's called the second sight but finding things is really thinking beyond the most obvious place, going a bit further."

May and I walked around the campus — not quite the historic playing fields I was used to but May especially liked the opportunity we had to go sailing on the lake. I canoed as if back on the Thames, the only thing that made me feel pleasantly homesick.

"It's not like a school," May said, "more a rather exclusive holiday club with a few useful mind games thrown in to keep us from getting bored. And there are some interesting people to talk to too, the kind Grimsi and I can do business with."

I began to feel confident that I had made a good decision coming here.

"I'll have to take time off on Mondays to go and check up on him," she said.

"Are you sure Grimsi is a good idea? Does your mentor approve?"

"I'm doing my Daddy's work."

What my work would be was still a great big empty question mark. A spacious, fully equipped, gentleman's study in London, as yet void of meaning, was waiting for me to give it new life. I envied May her certainty. And Roger! He was resisting the obligation to follow Dadi Hein in the highly successful manufacture of precision instruments — but it was there for him when he wanted it.

I got the name Conrad from my great-grandfather, my Dad's grandfather who had looked after him during the war when his mother and father were doing war work. Grandfather Conrad had war work too but he did it at home, interpreting the news from Russia, especially financial. He was really a private banker only his partner died when their offices were destroyed in the Blitz. I never knew him but I suppose Dad expected me to be a financial genius too.

I wasn't!

Or at least not beyond common sense.

When I had asked Dad how he did it, he said he just guessed, which I suppose is much the same thing. He said he got a beating at school for getting the right answers by guessing. The maths master insisted he write down his calculations to prove it, but he said he couldn't be bothered — actually he didn't know how. The headmaster's wife gave him tea and chocolate éclairs and let him play her piano. He invited her to his wedding as a thank-you.

I wondered if perhaps I too belonged in the money world. Mum's Dad had gambled big-time on the stock market — the Tinker, Dad called him because his initial fortune had been made as a scrap merchant — so I felt lucky to have the influence of my artist grandfather as well. He said he painted his clients as medievals did saints, not striving for a likeness but with revealing attributes, jockeys with horses is obvious but also the mean ones clutching ledgers in a tight grip, and others dressed up as country gentlemen but with more or less crooked ties. Nice people he left just sitting there looking nice.

Dad used to laugh at him for being a middle-class Tyneside socialist but I admired his judge of character and hoped I'd be something more like him.

Roger came to Geneva to see us — by train. The temptation of the Porsche hadn't worked.

"I'm moving to Zürich in September," he said. "As far away as I can get from my mother. Not that anywhere is far in Switzerland."

"You can visit me in Bern," said May. "That's even less far. I've been to Zürich by train with Grimsi — he had to collect cash from a client and needed a bodyguard."

Roger and I made our usual "girls!" face at each other.

"Dadi complains that I'm keeping him from retiring," Roger went on, "not that it hinders him really. With Mami managing the office he can take as much time off as he likes. He has taken up bird-watching. It gives him the chance to compare binoculars with the other birders and tour all the optics shops to look at telescopes. Mami can't understand it. He goes off with his fellow fanatics to spend hours doing nothing — as she sees it."

"Like fishing," said May.

"But she prefers it to when he went skiing with Smiley. That, she says, used to be much, much worse. Dadi Hein and Smiley made a dangerously reckless partnership, Smiley would pilot Dadi up the remoter slopes, dropping him off to find his way down alone while Smiley went ridge-rolling and stunt flying through gorges. She feared one or both might never return."

"Is that what the landing strip was for?" I asked.

"I was sorry when he sold the Pilatus Porter," said Roger. "I'd like to fly it myself."

"We'll buy a new one," said May.

The usual ganging up!

"My mother hated it," said Roger. "But in spite of that, she really loved Smiley. Not that he smiled much, hardly ever in fact, putting on a typically earnest Swiss act, but he made Dadi laugh — a lot. That's why I was happy when he came, he put them both in a marvellous good humour. They tried to persuade him to come and work with Hein again but he wouldn't, he said he was making plenty of money on his own, he didn't need partners to trip him up."

"Sounds like my Dad," I said.

"Or mine," said May.

Roger joined in with us laughing even if he didn't quite understand the joke of why we compared fathers, so similar and yet so different.

"Oh, damn it," I said, "I've got to bring him back. I've been practicing my Spanish on one of the Argentine guys here — arrogant twat that he is. God help me if they are all like him."

"Totenkopf has dealings with some Argies," said May. "Extravagant without having the gold to back it up. Grimsi says we got it all off them last time round. I'll check them out for you."

I had my doubts about how safe it was to get involved with Totenkopf's clients — but maybe it was the less reliable that I needed, or reliable in the Smiley sense of the word.

Having discussed fathers and futures, the next thing was that Uncle Paul came to see us.

"I pulled a thousand strings to be part of a commission in Geneva," he said. "I did it to set your mothers' minds at rest. I'll be busy but if you need me I'll be your problem-solver."

"I've got Grimsi," said May, unwilling to admit she might need my Uncle Paul. She liked him — everyone did, he was deceptively amiable — but she hadn't had him always as part of her life the way I had, even though he was one of her mother's ex-lovers before the Divine Sibyl settled on Uncle Gus, Paul's best friend from School. Paul had begun living on the top floor in our house when a student at LSE, but now Dad wasn't there any more he and Aunt Madge stayed on in the house for Mum's sake.

Aunt Madge worked as a free-lance financial advisor. She drove around to the various businesses and offices, whose muddles she sorted out, in her Renault 4 Plein-Air protected by her bulldog sprawled on the back seat. He sat up and scowled if anyone came too near, an effective burglar deterrent, even in London. Madge complained that living at the top of the house was bad for his joints but he didn't mind, he was used to it. Now he was getting old Madge wanted to put in a lift for him; she and Mum discussed it every so often. When the twins were small he used to guard them but now they were big he didn't bother, instead his main occupation when off duty was dosing in the shade beside Mum's aviary. Her hunting peregrine just stared back at him.

Uncle Paul, though not wanting to be our father-figure, liked his role as uncle. About once a month he took me to the theatre. He had ambitions to be a playwright. He also had an epic poem on the go that he'd scribble notes for but he wouldn't tell us what it was about. "A kind of Canterbury Tales" was all he'd say — but I deduced it was based on the Divine Sibyl's bizarre love-life. But really he had no time to be a poet.

"A life of contemplation would suit me," he said as he bustled around being diplomatic.

May didn't come with us, she said she got enough culture having to go and discuss Molière and trying to fathom Klee with her school group. At first I went just to please my uncle, not expecting much in Geneva beyond endless Ibsen, but then I joined the drama group and found I had a surprising talent for role playing. I always got nice parts to act, they said I was no good as a villain though I tried to look evil by brushing my eyebrows into pointy peaks like Dad's when he narrowed his eyes down to fiercely penetrating slits. It made the whole meaning of theatre more comprehensible.

We had a weekend free from sport and culture once a month. As May was in the *maturité* class she had the same freedom as the rest of us older pupils and made full use of it, as well as continuing her frequent trips to Totenkopf.

We regarded the Heinihof as our home. It was easy to get to by train and the Heins kept an indestructible old 4x4 Méhari at the station for ferrying up and down to the chalet. Any of us could take it. Even May. The key was left under the floor mat — as Roger would say, in Switzerland stealing cars in the mountains is not done.

Roger was doing his stint in the *Armee* and he too came for a weekend whenever he could. He didn't like to go home and have Dadi Hein overloading him with advice and instructions, so Mrs Hein came to the Heinihof to see him.

Uncle Paul remembered her from Mum and Dad's wedding and she remembered him as a school-boy.

"You kissed me," he reminded her. "That earned me £10, I had a wager with my new brother-in-law that I'd get £10 for every girl I coaxed a kiss out of. You were stunning and lovely to dance with."

"And you were a cute boy in your Eton suit."

Paul groaned. "Don't remind me. I was so embarrassed that Mother wouldn't buy me a smart grown-up suit for the occasion."

It was funny to realise that sharp Mrs Hein was one of the girls who had kissed Paul at the wedding. This was a story Mum and Paul often laughed over when they were reminiscing but I had always pictured the 'girls' being like May, not glamorous women like Mrs Hein. I could imagine myself kissing May for a wager or a forfeit, but Mrs Hein? I'd die!

Roger was making a face at the idea of Paul kissing his mother, but he needn't have worried. Paul was an easy-going husband firmly in Aunt Madge's clutches. God help any woman who tried to snaffle him!

"I'm so bored eating sausage and rösti, spaghetti and meat balls," said Roger. Army food was getting him down. "Let's go to the Palace for a good dinner."

"I'll cook dinner if you like," I offered though I hadn't actually ever prepared a whole meal before. Mum was useless in the kitchen but my Dad had been a good cook and I had often perched on a high stool to watch while he told me what he was doing, with funny stories in between. He could keep up a monologue for hours. I'd never forget what he told me. So I was quite eager to have a go at following in his footsteps.

"A little pig," said May, "with ears and a tail."

"I don't think Migros stretches to whole pig," said Roger. "But a few fat chops wouldn't be bad."

"And I'll do a tomato and onion salad," said May, "the way my Mama does.

Do you remember when your Dad did a pig on his birthday in the *casino* kitchen?"

"What is this casino?" asked Roger.

"A casino is a little house," said May, as if being patient with Roger's ignorance. May had spoken Italian in childhood and though she didn't any more she sprinkled Italian words around in conversation. "That's what Con's Dad used to call our villa to annoy my step-father Gus. Gus didn't mind his teasing, they were best friends really."

Tricky. That's what Gus called Dad but the way he said it, it was almost a compliment.

"The villa is nicely Italianate but Gus and his father also own a grim old tower no one could possibly live in. They keep arguing about what to do with it. I tell them that my Daddy would let it to a film producer who could blow it up for a dramatic climax. Then they could build some stylish houses on the land and make some useful money — if Daddy would only come back he'd do it for them."

May and I went down to Migros to buy what we needed for our dinner. I choose two chickens I could joint and grill the way my Dad did, and a bag of wild mushrooms certified by the local witch against poison — May's interpretation of the scrap of paper attached. May filled a bag with her salad ingredients, then we walked along the cobbled street to the dairy shop for a variety of cheeses and a slab of fresh butter, cream, and some quince jelly.

A fine feast even if nothing like the fancy food Roger could have had at the Palace!

"But better!" said Roger as he tucked in with me and May, Uncle Paul and his mother around him, a somewhat disjointed family but a happy one.

At home for the summer break I spent a large part of the time sitting at Dad's desk with the balcony doors open to the square and sparrows chirping in the trees, constructing in words and drawings my scenario of the grim tower with its blazing climax: a Tudor castle shedding a few stones while flames burst out through the windows; a cheering mob celebrating the end of feudal tyranny, leaving only the mild-mannered Uncle Gus in his Kentish-Palladian villa dealing with the white-collar crimes and misdemeanours of his peers.

The elegant symmetry of the plot kept me entranced — I'd get Uncle Paul to write the script. Red Roger with his attractive Swiss-English voice would be the roundhead republican hero doing his William Tell act. Not May but her far more romantically beautiful sister Augusta the Goose would be the heroine he would rescue from her world of ringletted kings and ermine befurred fathers.

As my demolition of despotic power progressed, the little green light winking at me, with an occasional outburst of red from a secondary device as punctuation mark, seemed signals of approval from somewhere out there in space.

I imagined my row of lights leaping into action and expanding into a meaningful existence, making sense in an enlightened society.

When I described it to the Sibyl she said:

"You're learning more from being in Geneva than just lessons in a classroom."

By September Roger was in Zürich, May, with her mentor's approval, was taking flying lessons on Saturdays, so my free week-ends were spent with Paul *zum Heinihofli*. We wandered over mountain paths or sat at a table overlooking the valley and the ridge of Oberland peaks beyond, plotting our drama. Paul enjoyed discussing the political and philosophical background with me even if he didn't take my enactment as a seriously practical proposition — any more than he seriously expected he himself would ever become the English Aristophanes.

"You do realise that if you spend your crazy father's inheritance on producing this you'll be penniless and lose the advantage he left you — I hope he didn't have any money in Buenos Aires because if so it will have been wiped out in the currency crisis."

"I'll find out next year when I go there," I said.

"You'll be lucky!" said Paul, deeply sceptical.

Worried by Paul's comment on Dad's money, I asked my irritating class-mate Pepe to explain their currency crises to me. However, it seemed just as incomprehensible to him as to me but he tried to make sense of it, saying every time when hyperinflation became hyper-hyper-inflation the bank introduced a new currency, so 1.000.000 pesos became 1 peso of a different name, and earnings and savings acquired a new value that left everyone con-fused and inevitably worse off than before. Pepe had a casual approach to money. During the war his mother's cousin had come in an Italian steamer across the Atlantic to Genoa and on to Switzerland to represent the beef exporters. I found myself having to explain why to Pepe, that the Swiss frank was the only currency that they could safely deal in, exchanging Argentine gold for franks to trade with other neutral nations, that's why he was now in a position to pay for Pepe's education. But Pepe didn't really appreciate it, he longed to go home and I realised his tiresome arrogance was merely salvaging the pride of a nation that had squandered its riches.

"When you go home," I said, "can I go with you?"

I explained that I wanted to find my father's burial place and bring him home to my mother. In my eagerness I started trying to explain my Dad, an exuberant man with overabundant love to give and, though my mother was the wife he respected and adored, his women-troubles had been the subject of endless funny stories. Even as a child I was freely part of his aud-ience when he held forth on the cruelty of women — not that anyone took his complaints seriously. He was much loved and forgiven his trespasses. The only one who voiced his disapproval was his father, our artist but non-Bohemian Grandfather. Our mother preserved a dignified silence on the subject. She deserved to have him returned to her.

Pepe didn't think it a feasible project any more than Paul and the Divine Sibyl, nevertheless said he'd be happy to invite me to visit his family. After that he regarded me as his best friend, which made me feel obliged to invite him for a week-end *zum Heinihofli*. I didn't want to let him in on our Drama so feared it would be a wasted week-end if Paul and I couldn't go on working on it. Paul didn't mind though and put Pepe through a thorough grilling on current affairs. Paul himself hadn't been back to South America, embarrassed by his failed attempt eight or nine years ago, but he was the one who knew about the woman who claimed she knew what had happened. So he was my hope for finding her and he saw that Pepe could be a help, however reluctant I was to trust him.

"They are all unreliable dodgers," Paul said. "You just have to make allowances for that. The people of every country are formed by their collective history but each person has their individual point of view. Ask questions and listen but it would be tactless to offer your own opinions; you don't know how his parents and grandparents may have been involved. The main thing will be to trace this woman known only by the name of Mirta and I seem to remember that she lived in the Palermo district. Not a lot to go on."

Nevertheless I felt buoyantly optimistic as knowing even half a name and a particular city district made her suddenly more real.

May and I flew home together for Christmas. When May was satisfied with tilting her seat up and down to the annoyance of the passenger behind her, she said: "Roger is getting his pilot's licence. He takes me up with him when I go to Belp to meet him. When he has his degree we are going to buy an old Porter-6 together so we can do what my Daddy did: bush flights into Africa. Grimsi is really excited about it because then he needn't bother any more about export and import licences."

Just as I feared: they were ganging up on me. And I'd have to put up with that all through the holidays.

While the twins were being the innocents with the monks in the Monastery of the Holy Innocents, Mum and I were going to stay at the *casino* with the Sibyl and Gus, and Joe with Grandfather in the gate-house so they could talk Art.

I remembered my Dad's birthday and the midnight feast he organised, the last one we had all together. It had taken place in the *casino's* vaulted octagonal kitchen on the ground floor, the pantries and wine-cellar that opened off in the four corners crammed with lovely food and drink. This plan repeated the architecture of the *piano nobile* above with the reception rooms opening off its central hall — including a formal dining-room that was used only when Uncle Gus received his professional connections, colleagues or the less evil of his clients — some of whom even Uncle Gus, who was the most open-minded man on earth, considered beyond the pale. That birthday party on the 1st of June 1980 was when Grandfather decided to stop having his studio with us in London and move down to Kent to join the Sibyl's magic circle, so May and her sister and brothers had the benefit of his regular company instead of us, his official grandchildren.

The architecture of the *casino* imposed a hierarchy of bedrooms from very grand: Uncle Gus's and the Sib's, Willie's, the guest-room where Mum slept, to a middling one each for May and The Goose, to the kind of quirky cupboard of a room occupied by Felix the latecomer, though it was a cupboard with a magnificent view. As children I had always shared with May because we used to play our fantasy games together until we fell asleep. Now I didn't know what to expect so I just sat on in the kitchen after supper and waited. Willie came and sat down beside me with a book of quizzes and puzzles and we took turns solving them. Willie was the same age as our twins, but not a bit silly, a really clever and nice little boy with a dense mop of dark curls. I had to ask myself how he'd feel about blowing up his ancestral tower. It seemed a pity for Willie's sake, no matter how grim. But maybe if we let him press the button to set off the dynamite he wouldn't mind. I'd have to think of a good part for him, better than the usual go-between played by such boys. He'd have to be a hero though we might have to kill him off tragically to make people cry.

But I wasn't pleased to think I might have to share a room with a thirteen-year-old — though big, it was largely occupied by a very complicated railway system with bridges and tunnels, not a place to blunder around in the dark.

May and Goosie came in to see if there was any cake left. So we sat around eating cake for a bit. Then Goosie said:

"Would you like to come and share my room for a change?"

"He's mine," said May.

"I can have a turn with him," said Goosie.

My heart did that clichéd thing of skipping a beat. In the year or more since I'd last seen the Goose, she had changed from a sweet child into the most gorgeous girl I had ever seen. I couldn't imagine anything more breath-takingly delightful than spending a night alone with her — but I simply couldn't trust myself not to lose my head and do something grossly indecent.

My Dad had started on his career as lover at eighteen but that was with an older woman, a kind of Mrs Hein who was well able to look after herself, not an adorable girl, the Divine Sibyl's younger daughter.

May repeated, "He's mine,"

No arguing with May.

Goosie gave me another heart-stopping smile and went off upstairs with Willie.

I sat in a daze trying to gather my wits while May phlegmatically cleared up the cake crumbs. Without further discussion I followed her upstairs.

"Do you remember," she said, coming back from the bathroom ready for bed...

Oh, damn it! I thought, she's so grown-up since the last time I was here...

"when we used to play...

It's the Geneva sophistication and all that flying around with Roger — not to mention Grimsi, who knows what goes on there...

"at mothers and fathers?"

Damn it, damn it! Not that!

"You were such an inquisitive boy, you used to spy on your dicey Dad when he was doing his thing, remember that time here in Dr Johnson's tea-house with my Mama, and you said you'd show me how they did it...

"That must have been the time they made Felix," I said hoping to deflect the discussion on to this interesting topic. "Neither she nor Uncle Gus will admit it, but it's perfectly obvious where she got him: he's not a bit like Willie, and the fire-cracker hair and that little lippy, pouty mouth..."

"... just like yours, he must be your brother... We tied ourselves in knots with legs all over the place but you couldn't get it in."

"For pity sake, we were children."

"I laughed at you and you were so cross you'd never try it again."

May was still laughing. I could see where this was going. It wasn't my heart that was jumping about...

"Well," I said, "if you are thinking of trying again now, I probably still can't."

Wrong move. I'd laid myself open to check.

"You're seventeen, you must be well able by now."

Checkmate! It would be rude to say I'd prefer to try with Goosie, and besides, even so, sitting on the side of the bed in my shirt and under-pants with a shapely young female beside me, my cock was telling me it was time to give it another go.

It was happening even while I was arguing with myself about the propriety of getting it up with May, my life-long companion who also conveniently happened to be a girl.

It was easy for me, it was May who struggled a bit. But she made me press on, determined to complete the process, until I reached a rather splendid climax inside her.

"I shouldn't have done that," I said, shocked and ashamed of giving in to her. "We don't need another Felix."

"Of course not," said May, "I'm not stupid. Was it nice for you?"

"Actually, yes, very."

"Good, then we have the rest of Christmas to perfect our technique."

This was such typical May-speak I attached no importance to her meaning, being more than ready to try again. And she was right, it got better the more we practiced, which we did several times in the course of the next four days. It was marvellously satisfying and gave me a terrific sense of well-being and confidence. The one snag was that the more I did it with May, the more I longed to make it an outpouring of true love with sweet Goosie.

Getting ready to go home, while Joe was fussing over loading his gear into Mum's car, Goosie came sidling up to me and said, "You let May hog you, spending all that time in her room and not once visiting me, you mean thing."

"I didn't know you wanted me to," I said, too embarrassed to admit my own feelings. "Anyway, you're too young for that."

"You could at least kiss me," she said.

I took her hand and we fled across the hall into Uncle Gus's Archive crammed with books and pictures, and under the *memento mori* portrait of my Dad, I kissed my blossoming sweetheart to my heart's content. But only when they were shouting for me to come and get in the car did my last hug descend into a plump little pussy tickle before I ran out the front door. When I looked back at the house she was watching me from the Archive window with her lips squashed against the glass.

I sat beside Mum all the way home with my heart pounding fit to burst.

When we were in the plane back to Geneva, May said:

"That was a great holiday."

I agreed.

"You did a splendid job in getting my molly working smoothly. I was nervous that if Roger wanted to do it with me he'd find me sticky going. Now I'm ready for anything. Thanks."

If I hadn't spent that half hour kissing and cuddling my darling girl I'd have been furious with May's frank abuse of my affectionate fucking. As it was, I too smiled in contentment over a successful Christmas holiday.

It was amazing what a difference those four days intense work-out between May's lovely strong legs made to my life. Sometimes I felt I was bursting out of my skin I was so happy. I studied hard all day and held inane conversations with fellow students in various languages. That way I was able to make myself save up the blissful sensations of kissing my sweetheart for the night hours when I was alone with my memory and imagination. Now I knew the real-life marvel of making love with May it was not difficult to put Goosie in her place. Every night I fell asleep embracing her and woke in the wintery dawn brimming over with zest for the day.

Since May's language studies were to improve on Grimsi's Bernese German and reactivate her Italian, and mine were more serious French and Spanish, and her mathematics were scientifically biased and mine simple accountancy, the only classes we shared were English, so it wasn't too hard to keep out of her way. I honestly didn't want our friendship to be messed up with random sex.

Paul had gone to Australia with Aunt Madge to spend Christmas there in the scorching heat with her brother. They weren't back yet but I was looking forward to our first free week-end as a chance to be peacefully alone in the *Heinihof*. I was quite surprised when May said she was coming with me.

"Are you not flying?" I asked.

"I've done enough for the time being," she said. "I'll start again when the weather is better."

"Is Roger coming?"

I certainly didn't want to be present as the third man.

"I don't know," she said. "I don't think so. Does it matter?"

I could have thumped her for her obtuseness.

"Of course it matters. I can't work if you two are cavorting around."

"We don't cavort. Are you jealous?"

"Have I reason to be?"

May shrugged and walked away from me, but on Friday she was there ready to go, all muffled up in long coat and fur hat like a proper lady — which was just as well as when we got to our station it was snowing, getting dark and the Méhari wasn't there.

"Even if Roger or someone has the car up at the chalet they won't want to come down for us and risk getting stuck in a blizzard," I said. "We'll go to the Palace for the night."

I felt immensely proud escorting Mistress May into the grandeur of the Palace and engaging a room for us, a junior suite facing south so we could wake up late in the morning and with luck see the sun sparkling on the snowy roofs of the town below and the mountain behind. If I had planned this it would never have worked out so well.

We had *quenelles de brochet* for supper with wine from Valais, and rhum baba with Bourbon vanilla ice-cream, so we went glowing with heat and fine food, up to our huge downy bed. It felt as if our love bouts in May's room at home had been rehearsals, tuning up our instruments for this, our gala performance.

It was pointless to think I might have preferred a different mouth to kiss, different hands to caress me. Love would have another dimension when I had my sweetheart with her meltingly tender pussy in my arms, but in the here and now it was glorious hot May I had to give my love to and it was me, not the hero Roger, that she was urging on.

"Come on, cock of my cunny, get in here and do your stuff," she said, wrapping her legs around me.

Oh, blessed love, that comes in many guises to delight us!

And my brave cock, tried and tested and proved fully functional!

I phoned the *Heinihof* in the morning to find out who was there. It was Mr and Mrs Hein who had come for a week's skiing. Even though the hotel reception said we could have our suite for the second night at a reduced rate, which to me was an attractive proposition, for May the attraction of getting to know Mr Hein, whom we had met only briefly once before, was too great to waste time dallying around with me.

"He was the owner of the Pilatus Porter bush plane my Daddy used to fly into Africa," she said. "Maybe I can get him to buy another for Roger to fly for us when Grimsi and I need some extra special delivery done."

I groaned but held my tongue. This was all outside my sphere of influence and anything I said would only reveal my petty jealousy. After all, if May were using me as a substitute for Roger, it ought to be no worse than having her beat me at chess in our earlier confrontations. She would always have the advantage of being the Divine Sibyl's daughter. My Dad hadn't married darling Mum for her brains; her beauty and serene disposition were what he adored and cherished...

... as I would adore and cherish my sweet, lovely, madly desirable Goosie.

I felt an adult understanding of my Dad, the affection he had for the women who loved him and the immense pleasure he had in making love to them, how that didn't diminish his love for his wife but enhanced it. And *visa versa*. With that in mind I wanted to hug May but she had no patience for casual shows of affection, however vigorously she responded in bed.

"Do you see any snow-buntings around here?" May asked Mr Hein at the earliest opportunity.

"No, but..." and he launched himself into an account of the local bird-life. She had him hooked.

I smiled to myself with pride in her ability to get what she wanted. She sat with him on the balcony with his second-best binoculars, hoping to catch sight of some passing speciality, while I occupied myself with helping Mrs Hein around the house, even submitting to her inquisition about Mum's manner of surviving in widowhood. She seemed slightly disappointed to hear that in spite of Dad's absence Mum's financial strength remained constant and caused her no worries.

"Those still reserves! He always had a good head for money, the wily bastard, even with his colossal risk-taking. Your mother is lucky it came off — so far, but don't count on his house of cards not to come crashing down eventually."

"I don't think so," I said. I was determined not to let her rile me, to betray neither Dad nor Mum however adversarial she made it sound. "Whatever happens, the London property will go on paying. It is not going to collapse. Mum will continue well able to support her mother, her charities and her hobbies."

"And no doubt her expensive children. Is it true he left her with twins to add to her burden of worries?"

"She absolutely adores the twins. Joe and I could be jealous, she spends far more time fussing over them than she ever did over us, but actually we don't, we're pleased she has them to keep her happy."

"Are they like your father?"

"It's hard to say really, they have gingery blond hair, not really red, and they are quite extraordinarily beguiling, Grandfather says much like Dad was at that age. He prophecies trouble when they hit puberty, but no sign of it so far."

"Probably not," said Mrs Hein, relenting in her critical attitude, "after all they have your nice mother to bring them up, not like your dreadful grand-mother who from all accounts thoroughly neglected your poor father. He was lucky to survive with no one but his crazy old grandfather to look after him."

"He didn't believe in luck and said he was very happy as a child."

"Well, we'll see."

She spoke as if she were a privileged audience of one enjoying the comedy of our family drama. I'd certainly tell her nothing of my own plans. It was none of her business.

Mrs Hein and I joined the other two with coffee on the balcony, Mrs Hein wrapping herself in furs to bask in the sun behind the barricade of window boxes which were now stripped of their red and white tea towels, showing their buds of spring green. May had led Mr Hein away from bird to mechanical flight and was asking him leading questions about his old Pilatus Porter 6, its equipment and instruments.

"What about the time my Daddy flew it?" she asked.

Mr Hein gave his little laugh — he was given to little sniggers and giggles, as if everything amused him, untouched by the troubles of the common herd — then he sighed.

"He was the best, especially navigation, he had a contour map of the world in his head. When I lost him I lost interest in flying. I'm pleased that Roger is keeping the spark alive."

"I'm not," said Mrs Hein from the depths of her muffles. "The last thing I want is Roger imitating that madman. You should never have encouraged him, Heini darling. It's all your fault."

Mr Hein laughed. "He defied every challenge I threw at him. He was a run-away, wild boy until we took him in hand. We were the making of him."

"I saved him from the machine-hall girls," said Mrs Hein. "He was only too willing to let them play games with him. He'd have had them all up the spout if we hadn't put a stop to it."

"I had you to thank for that, dear," said Mr Hein, "he had the whole typing-pool in a state of sex-fuelled turmoil while acting the innocent himself," then dismissing the question of the girls, he added, "He was on the run from the Queen of England..."

"Until we made a proper little Switzer of him."

Something both the Heinses thought hilariously funny.

"I have a Swiss passport," said May. "My Daddy got it for me in Bern even though I was born in London. Grimsi says it's a good thing."

May didn't often express uncertainty but evidently Grimsi's approval was important. It showed that she too was a proper little Switzer.

The four of us went skiing in the afternoon and in the evening Heini made us his special fondu, main ingredients Emmentaler, Vacherin and Kirsch, with a sprinkling of fennel seeds. I had avoided fondu knowing Dad's dislike of excessive cheesiness, but this one was nice, a bulwark against falling on one's nose in the snow. As I ate I was thinking how I could get the same satisfying smooth cheesiness in a less stolid form, something fluffy and creamy and delicious, but when I tried to describe it to Mrs Hein, she said: "Clever boy, it sounds as if you've just re-invented the Soufflé Suissesse."

Why does she dislike me so much? I asked myself, resolving once again not to be provoked by her jibes. She had called me "the Angel's boy" which suggested it was my mother whom she hated. The only thing anyone could dislike in Mum was that she was too good, too beautiful, too kind — and that my Dad loved her with all his generous, witty, wildly extravagant heart. Was that the clue? I'd ask Roger when I got the chance — Roger seemed to love his mother with a self-protective reserve, safer at a distance. Perhaps a strategy learnt in childhood, Smiley's way.

I stood up and wished the Heinses good night, thanking them for a lovely day. May did likewise and I put my arm around her shoulders in an unthinking gesture of defiance, feeling pleasure that we were standing here together, gleefully defying convention in spite of Heini's giggles and Mrs Hein's antagonism. I was proudly aware of my own strength — and, what was more, the Angel's boy was an inch or more taller than Mrs Hein's Roger.

"Let's do it in Roger's room," said May, copying the Heini snigger.

"So you can imagine it's Roger tickling you fanny," I said, but I wasn't really cross about it.

"I think Roger would be more of a romantic lover," she said.

'I'll do my best," I said, ready for anything with May in skittish mood, cock jumping for joy at the prospect of a good work-out. Happiness is a hot cock! And the exercise May gave it kept it humming. Oh glorious May! She was not a romantic lover either, but then, neither of us was in love. We were comrades who had grown up sharing experiences — and this was ultimately the best of them.

In the morning Heini's giggle expressed his amusement at our juvenile indiscretions and Mrs Hein relapsed into her more malicious mood. But the only outcome was that after a late breakfast of croissants from the freezer and sweet goats cheese with blueberries, Mrs Hein said frostily that she's drop us off at the station on her way to meet a friend for lunch at the Palace. Nevertheless, she kissed us both good-bye, saying to me, "Give my regards to your Uncle Paul, I hope he'll be back from Australia soon — how terribly inconvenient of him to marry an Australian —" and to May she said, "You are so very like your beautiful mother. Take care!"

When we were in the train, May said to me, "What on earth did she mean by that? I'm not a bit like my mother."

"She was probably thinking of the Divine Sibyl luring a succession of lovers to murder and mutilation. Everyone knows that. Only Uncle Gus is immune to her, like looking at the Medusa through a mirror. That's why she married him. And Heini probably thinks sixteen is too young to be going down the same path."

"Well, you're not much older," said May. She never let me take advantage of my less than a year's seniority. "Mama was nineteen when she met my Daddy and I was the result of that first encounter with sex. That's why she tells me not to leave it to chance but make responsible decisions."

"Am I a responsible decision?"

"Of course, triple A, my Daddy would approve. He'd approve of Roger too, only Roger isn't forthcoming — yet."

"I've no intention of being a threesome with Roger," I said as decisively as I could to impress on her that she'd have to choose, though I was less certain than I sounded, knowing how hard it was to say no to May.

I bought a beautiful postcard of the lake with the fountain and wrote to the Divine Sibyl:

"This is such a great school, May and I are doing really well, why not send Goosie over to join us. There's a very good music department if that's what she'd like."

I put it in an envelope for the sake of discretion.

Divine phoned back.

"What do you really want? Whatever about the school, all May talks about is the good time she has flying with Roger, and now it seems she has the great Heini at her bidding. Wise move: always get the father on your side. Are you feeling left out?"

I was tongue-tied. I didn't dare tell her that actually it was me who had full-on sex with May, not Roger, but her Sibylline instinct was right in supposing that it was really her younger daughter I was aching for, that I couldn't get over that kiss, indelibly registered for all time in Uncle Gus's hallowed Archive. I could truthfully promise to respect my precious sweetheart but would she trust me? Could I trust myself?

The Divine Sibyl's answer was no.

I was still brooding over the Sibyl's refusal when May met me on my way back from the canoe shed and fell into step beside me. Pleasantly tired and sweaty as I was from a few hours on the lake, dick-down-below's automatic response was to start stirring up trouble, no matter how inappropriate in our school environment.

"This weekend Roger is trying out an old Pilatus Porter like his Dadi had. We are going to take it up to the *Heinihof* — he got the gardener to give the landing strip a good clearance. He might buy it if it's any good. Would you like to come with us?"

I was both surprised and pleased to be asked. It seemed safe enough, though I was careful to avoid situations where Roger and I could become rivals.

"Only if it's strictly business — no sex."

May laughed at me.

"You're the one who will have to keep a firm hold on your frisky cock. Roger and I get enough thrill out of flying."

From that I deduced that the red-heads hadn't committed incest. My tall, blond mother had saved me from that, so, relieved of that worry, I looked forward to a flight over the mountains.

I cooked dinner while May and Roger put their heads together over the details of how they rated the deal with the PP-6. Roger seemed satisfied enough but I noted that May was the sharper at calculating cost. In the meantime I considered the choice in the freezer. The result of my efforts was a perfectly delicious choucroute with pork tenderloin in chunks in addition to the inevitable sausages. It merited a word of appreciation from Roger though May dismissed it with:

"My Daddy never cooked anything so bourgeois."

"Maybe not," I said, "but my Dad was adept at making the best of whatever was available, food or..."

"Lovers," said May.

"If you like, that too."

I wasn't going to enter into a discussion with May about the significance of the best. When May and I made love we were both using the best available — which was actually very good indeed, like a satisfying plate of Wienerli on a bed of sauerkraut, the best of its kind, appropriate to the occasion.

May decided she would sleep in state in Mrs Hein's bed and departed, leaving Roger and me to go up to the games room under the roof where we played a few rounds of billiards, which Roger won easily, then we lay down on two of the couches that were there to serve as occasional beds, mainly for the ski parties Heini organised for his office staff.

After Roger gave me an account of his engineering course —

"We're probably among the most well-heeled bunch of students in the world," he said, laughing at himself, "but we can't admit it, we have to grumble and protest, like graffiti we have to do what we can — always within reason — to deface such utter perfection or we'd become altogether too smug..."

— we got talking about our schools, and discovered that though on the face of it Roger's Steiner education couldn't be more in opposition to the traditions of my ancient School, the outcome was much the same, an awareness and confidence in ourselves as individuals.

"Tomorrow we'll fly across the Eiger and maybe some day we'll climb it together," he said.

"I doubt it," I said. "Long-distance trekking is more my thing. I'm not too keen on the steeply vertical."

When we flew past the mountain peak and I saw close up what he proposed, I was even more certain I'd never be one of the vertically-obsessed. Dad wasn't either. For all his death-defying stunts, taking the most difficult way up a wall of rock only to come down again on the other side wouldn't strike him as worth the risk. Dodging storm clouds with a swag-bag of diamonds on the other hand...

I wondered if Roger had similar plans as he set course back to Belp. Roger's very Swissness made him hard to assess. He might abide strictly by the letter of the law, but just as likely he'd obstinately refuse to accept any authority he didn't agree with.

"Consensus," he'd say. "We exist by the laws we make for our own good."

Landing with Totenkopf's fortune in diamonds was probably not illegal when Dad did it, whatever about trade embargoes and export licences in the rest of the world.

I asked Pepe if he would be going home for Easter, but he said no, he couldn't, he'd have to spend it being homesick in an Alpine hut, acting guide to a bunch of Argie exiles down from Paris, so I'd have to wait for the summer break to fulfil my plan. While I was pondering on how I was going to accomplish this, May passed her *maturité* exams and immediately flew off with Roger into the unknown. Mrs Hein was in a terrible state of anxiety until Roger phoned from Johannesburg to say he was taking a year off to work as a free-lance bush pilot and not to worry, that he'd be back to finish his degree course in Zürich, but he didn't say when. I said May wouldn't stay away from Grimsi for long, but that didn't make Mrs Hein any less anxious. However, Heini himself approved. He said it showed initiative and resourcefulness, exactly the qualities he appreciated in his heir for taking over the business. He rated a university degree less highly than the personal training he gave his apprentices.

"Look at Smiley, he learned everything he knew from working with me, but his fortune came from his own inventiveness and hard work."

I knew all along that all the flying practice was leading up to some ven-ture like this, and with Grimsi's backing they had the financial resources of *Totenkopf (Schweiz)* to support them. But soon I'd have the Baccalaureate safely to my credit and my eighteenth birthday, so I too was ready to take wings and tackle the world.

Before reaching a decision I flew home to the Sibyl.

I found her in her pillared hall surrounded by the gigantic Virtues glowering down from some *trompe-d'oeil* Italian Elysium, fresco colours happily now faded into muted blues and greens, only the earthy ochres and pinks withstanding the passage of centuries. The Divine One was sitting at

Dad's Steinway, not actually making music. She liked just to sit there, especially in times of stress, waiting for inspiration.

She smiled to see her expectation that I'd come fulfilled.

"I need you to go and find May for me," she said. "I'd go myself only I have Gus with Willy and Felix to consider, and I don't care to travel, this is my place."

Well yes, the Delphic Sibyl always stays put in her temple.

"I'd like you to remind her that she needs my permission to marry."

Marry?

"The dreadful Hein woman phoned me to say that on no account was my daughter to marry her son. She sounded quite out of her mind. I told her May is not insecure, she has everything she needs so she is unlikely to do something as silly as get married at seventeen. As far as I'm concerned, I said, they can go on living in sin in the black heart of Africa where no one gives a damn what they do. She said she shouldn't have expected anything better from a siren like me. So I'd like you to go and see May just to make sure."

"No," I said. "I'm not getting mixed up in that. Send Paul."

"Why not, you're their friend. Or are you jealous? Do you want May yourself?"

My dilemma! I had no choice but tell the truth.

"May and I are best friends and that includes sex, but we're not lovers. Not that I don't truly care for her as well, but... anyway, that she can't marry Roger has nothing to do with me."

"I've never met the Heini boy so I've no way of judging how suitable he is. I just don't want to lose May to that family, knowing the trouble it cost her father to escape them. I'm jealous — it's always been my weakness. Besides she really would be better off living in sin, even in Switzerland in spite of Mrs Hein. My God! Why would anyone want that woman as a mother-in-law?"

"Because Roger is terrific fellow, a bit like Dad the way he goes about everything with a frown, concentrating, only Roger is genuinely earnest, not laughing inside like Dad."

"'*Laughter at the foot of the cross*,' Gus used to call it," said the Sibyl. "His ironic laughter fought against the tragedies that haunted him all his life."

I was dumbfounded by this statement. So much so that I couldn't think what to make of it and went on with my own line of thought about May and Roger.

"May admires the splendid physique he has from all that tramping over mountains in big boots and a gun on his back, like Dad. He is so very much one of us, even though he did grow up in that weirdly strange country."

"May won't have any trouble dealing with the weirdly strange," said the Sibyl.

"As long as she doesn't marry it," I said, trying to add force to my words so she'd take me seriously. Then before I could stop myself I whispered: "I'll marry the Goosie if you'd let me. She wants me too."

I blushed and trembled as I remembered the little pussy eagerly rubbing up against my caresses. A sensation to die for!

The Divine Sibyl smiled tenderly. "The perfect childhood sweethearts. Of course you may, Con dear, you'll keep her safe from all the adventurers and lechers. But you can't for another two or three years. Gus has his lordly reputation to consider. "

"Are we not too closely related?"

"You're not related at all, that's the beauty of it. Goosie's father died for love. Such folly! He expected me to marry him but I choose Gus instead. Doing the dramatic Italian thing by falling — or being pushed — off a castle wall. His family want her, but you'll keep her away from them. There's no one I'd sooner trust her to."

Divine Sibyl! I was dizzy with joy and hugged her. I'd been a child in love with her all my life and I kissed her now with all the satisfaction of being a man. A whole new world of possibilities opened up for me.

But first things first.

"Now Paul is back I'm going to go on my quest to the River Plate and see for myself what can be done about Dad."

"Take care!" she said, in white-face Sibylline mode. "In 1971 your father did the same, searching for his mother in the French Caribbean. But that had nothing remotely like the difficulties you'll face."

"He succeeded," I said, encouraged that she reminded me of my unknown grandmother's equally mysterious disappearance — I hadn't even associated my quest with his, the one he made to find out why he'd been abandoned to survive as best he could aged only eleven — "admittedly what came back was only some bones and a skull with red hair, but if I achieve even that much it will be a triumph."

The Sibyl shuddered, with staring limpid blue eyes, not looking at me.

"It may be worse," she said. "He counted on his Swiss passport to keep him out of trouble, and the financial importance he had for both sides, but eventually something must have gone amiss. The possibilities were so awful, I suffered agonies, through intuition or telepathy — I could hear his voice calling to me. It was the worst time of my life and I still have nightmares. But do what you have to do. Maybe you can bring closure to his end, however dreadful."

Uncle Paul had said that our lovely Sibyl was a Cassandra, always expecting the worst, so I tried not to take her premonitions too anxiously.

But my dreams of love became confused, Sibyl's nightmares intruding into the happiness of embracing my sweet Goosie.

Paul, answering the Sibyl's appeal, reported back from South Africa that Roger and May had set up a small airfield with fairly basic equipment using as office a shack lent to them by one of Grimsi's connections, doing not only Totenkopf business but acting as transport and delivery service for another of his mad enterprises, *Maddie's Ethnic Lekkerbekken*.

"They are talking of expanding the field for safari and eco-tourists, so it doesn't look as if they'll be coming home any time soon. The Maddie of the Ethnic Food company is happy to have them there. She said she always regretted she couldn't persuade Totenkopf himself to stay and work with her, but now with Roger's backing she has registered her business under the Swiss flag, a sure guarantee of quality. It goes down especially well in Japan.

Roger bunny-hops the produce to JAL in Cape Town to ensure it arrives it prime condition.

My London office with its elaborate communication systems began to feel less directionless, warming up at the prospect of being the respectable cover address for a shack in de veldt somewhere around Witwatersrand. Dad and I used to play puzzle games and I was sure it was only a matter of time before I unlocked the riddle of his cryptic mindset, but instead of concentrating on the business on hand I found myself dreaming and day-dreaming about how it would work out living there with Goosie. Dad had Napoleon's narrow campaign bed to lie on when he wanted to be alone, or waiting for a phone call — he was never impatient, he could relax totally in whatever circumstances. I kept imagining varieties of lovely beds coming to take its place: lacy woven wicker frames, springy horsehair, pure white Polish goose-down, smooth St Gallen sheets patterned in tendrils of green, pink and purple passion flowers, a nest to shelter our love.

Napoleon's bed was really too short for me, if I stretched out fully my feet stuck out over the end. I never expected I'd be as tall as my Dad, but then I hadn't measured myself against him for a long time so I couldn't know. He used to give me a hand to let me climb up and stand balanced on his shoulders while he held me by the ankles, and he'd say that thing about a pigmy on the shoulders of a giant, so that's the image that stuck in my mind. Now I was six foot two and a half so I was already taller than it said he was on his (British) passport, the one in his safe together with his UK driving licence. I remembered when he and Mum were dressed up, how tall he looked in evening clothes, stiff black and white and a long dark overcoat, Mum all in silver including the silver fox fur he brought her from New York, how he arranged the fox up around her face — even as a child I could see the tenderness of his gesture, now I could feel it in my own hands, lips, eyes — and in her excessively high heels she was the taller. He loved her for it, proud of his goddess of a wife, stylishly sober, stunningly bejewelled. They were a perfect couple, and with Joe and me a model family. Sometimes May stood in beside us to make up the perfect number.

So height and grace were my birthright.

While I was consulting the Sibyl and trying out my office, Pepe had gone home without me. However, before I could get lost in dreams of love, he telephoned from the opposite side of the world.

"When are you coming over?"

"Now," I said.

To hell with the Doubting Thomases, I'd go it alone.

I tried to drag as much information out of Paul as I could but it proved extraordinarily difficult.

"I'd better come along," he said. "I can show you places more easily than describe how to find them. BA is a labyrinth. On the face of it a simple grid cut through with diagonals that are meant to make getting around quicker, until you try to get to one district from another and find yourself somewhere entirely different: instinct, not logic is what seems to work, or being blind like Borges."

That started off a whole clamour. Joe insisted I had promised to take him, then the twins decided they were coming too. Mum couldn't bear to see them go so she went down to Kent where she was a hindrance to the workings of the Sibylline intuition just when we needed it in top form. Grandfather promised to keep the second sight stimulated with a supply of magic mushrooms.

It nearly broke my heart to go away and leave the Goosie and our love unconsummated but I had to earn my reward and the Divine Sibyl was right to send me off, even if she didn't believe in my mission. She seemed to know already what the outcome would be.

"The least," I said, "I may get is a proper death certificate. That will make it simpler for May and me to take over without legal complications."

Mum and the Sibyl didn't want a death certificate, as if that would be a betrayal, a definite killing off of hope.

Saying goodbye, Sibyl hugged me to the divine bosom I'd been at liberty to nestle against as a child, and said, "Your Dad thought you the best little boy in the world, don't let him down."

"Was my Dad truly in love with you?"

Sibylla smiled.

"We never agreed about love."

"But I saw you. You were gorgeous and terribly sweet to him even when he moaned and complained that love was killing him."

"Dear little Connie, such a funny little boy, our spy in the house of love! I would have liked to keep you; I was so afraid you wouldn't be properly cared for but happily once the twins came along your mother stopped her flitting about and started to pay attention to your education. And see what a good job she has made of you. You'll do us proud."

I was enormously encouraged by the Sibyl's approval. There was nothing ambiguous about that whatever she thought the outcome would be.

I felt a bit foolish arriving in Buenos Aires not just with Paul to do a serious investigation, but with a following of 16-year-old Joe and the saintly twins Axie and Boris, thirteen, who were hoping to find the tomb of the saintly Evita. When our own Philippine Evita heard where they'd gone she came flying after them, which was a relief to us · why didn't we think of that ourselves? · as she could take charge of them doing pilgrimages, and with her Philippine Spanish manage to communicate fairly well with the Porteños, with the right degree of cheeky vulgarity: Evita was no chicken.

My Geneva friend Pepe was almost too eager to be helpful, Paul had to restrain him from talking too much and speculating too wildly. However, on the Sunday after our arrival we were pleased enough to be invited to an *asado* at his family home.

The party was assembled in an enclave of some stylish modern houses, sheltering behind high gates. Of the gathering of people wandering around like extras in a movie I never found out who belonged with which house and who were guests. Pepe was very casual with his introductions. Two years in Geneva hadn't been enough to teach him to look people in the eye and say their full name.

The twins of course made a big impression, holding court with Evita as interpreter. They handed her their School toppers — without which they had refused to travel — while organising the other youngsters to run 3-legged races, which naturally they won easily. Even when their Doppelgänger advantage was rumbled and they were asked to split up, they choose to partner the leggiest girls and still won. Delighted with their girl companions, they allowed them wear their toppers and the girls swopped them for suitably slouchy gaucho hats instead. The trouble from that arose only in September when they tried to go back to School as gauchos.

When asked what was the importance of covering their heads, if it were a religious practice, they said, yes, but actually it was to hide that they didn't have really, really red hair like their Dad. He used to call them his baby Gingermen. When Joe and I piled in on top of him and the babies he'd hug us all and boast, 'See what terrific balls I have that produced this lot!'

The twins stayed tied together at the ankles with the girls they called Tickles and Blimp for the rest of the day, communicating with digs and giggles, and when a bandoneón started to play they danced as a foursome, figuring out appropriate six-legged tango entanglements. A huge success.

Evita's other, more normal role in life, when not guiding the twins in their career as Holy Innocents, was as Old Father William's housekeeper. She'd been devoted to looking after him since, during a law case against a dealer, he got her de-toxed and cleaned up enough to appear as a credible witness, and so rescued her from her career as sex slave. Now, relieved of the clingy twins, she could join in with the other women doing the more menial work while the men attended the fires. I got a mild shock when inspecting the joints of meat laid out for cooking, trying to identify them — nothing like what one would buy in Migros — I put out a finger to taste what I thought was English mustard when Pepe indicated it was oozing out of some unidentifiable intestine which later, curled up and crispy from the grill, was actually quite nice to chew.

A row broke out when Evita objected to the father of one of the dancing girls making a video of the children.

"Para¡ para¡" she cried, "The twins are copyright!"

This caused considerable astonishment when she said all images of the miraculous twins belonged to Radio Manila.

Even I who had known them from birth, was disconcerted by this. Did Mum know her twins belonged to Manila Radio? Joe and I had often laughed at Great-Uncle Harold and his monks making an unholy fuss over them but now it appeared that Evita had a share in them as well.

Uncle Paul and Pepe's father, who had gone off to have a quiet talk, reappeared in time to pacify the situation, though Evita wasn't satisfied until she got Blimp's father to sign a form, which she had ready in her hand-bag, stating that images of the twins were for private viewing only and not for publication.

This enormously enhanced Evita's standing amongst the chattering women. Joe on the other hand was furious with the fuss, it was just so like his little brothers to steal the limelight! However, he allowed Pepe's sister to drag him into the dance and began to enjoy himself, though he was even happier when Pepe displayed an unexpected talent for singing tragic ballads and a deep melancholy descended on the evening.

Only the promise from the Tickles and Blimp mothers that they would take them swimming tomorrow persuaded the twins to let Evita untie them from their partners. It was actually the beginning of the twins becoming individuals. When Boris kissed Rosita's blimpish rosy cheek he stopped ever being Axie, and when Camilla tickled Axie's thirteen-year-old tummy he was not being Boris but truly himself.

Joe and Pepe took to sitting in bars around Palermo, Joe with his sketch-book doing portraits of the variety of strong, handsomely crooked, scarred faces while Pepe engaged people in conversations that might give a clue to a woman called Mirta. Dad had given a good description of her to Paul in what was probably their last talk before the phone calls ceased entirely: a Queen Mother who washed his Budd shirts in a stone sink in the yard of an elegantly decrepit townhouse and cooked him a Patagonian lamb to eat in the shade of a fig tree. Even if an Argentine Queen Mother were hard to imagine, Joe drew her portrait with all the details he could associate with Dad's description. He was so convinced by his own image of her he was sure he'd recognise her when he saw her, faded fake blond hair and all. In the meantime he was accumulating an excellent portrait gallery, which eventually ensured his acceptance at St Martins. The distinctive style of his Buenos Aires work rescued him from the accusation that his art was too derivative of his grandfather's.

Gradually Joe's persistence was rewarded as people began to admit they might remember whom he meant: a woman who used to hang out locally, but who hadn't been seen for a while.

In the meantime, Paul consulted the Swiss bank's representative, not the one he had met previously. He suggested we take the lift up a floor and talk to Ueli Mueller but didn't specify what this Mr Mueller's function was. Amongst these politely serious, self-confident men I felt myself growing up to be one of them. Though like May I was born in London and educated at the School of Schools until we opted for Geneva, her Daddy had chosen Swissness for her. Why hadn't my Dad done the same for me? I'd have felt a stronger claim to Mr Mueller's services, especially in such dubious circumstances. Paul of course had no such qualms, or doubts about his own identity to hold him back.

Mr Mueller had no new facts to report, but could fill in a few rumours about the red-head foreigner who had become quite familiar around town until his disappearance — in a city of disappearances.

"As one of us," said Mr Mueller, "he should have been reasonably immune from harassment, but it seems he antagonised the AID workers who were working with the police here, so-called development advisors doing nothing but stirring up trouble. My predecessor told you all he knew, but since then there have been more revelations — the ferry crossing and then this woman surfaced who claimed she knew for certain he'd been shot somewhere beyond Montevideo. We had only her word for it and she left no contact address."

Paul's eyebrow expressed doubt, so Mr Mueller added: "We didn't leave it at that, we sent a few local agents to fish around for any further evidence, but no one admitted seeing anyone answering that description."

"That's not very encouraging," I grumbled to Paul as we left the anonymous high-rise office building — how totally different from its medieval counterpart a similar South American shared with *Totenkopf* in Bern! "And, if he shaved his head and wore a cap, that red-head description would be useless."

Paul merely shrugged.

"He doesn't want us to think he should have done better. I'm sure they did all they could. In a population of only seven million every citizen counts, it would be a matter of national pride not to lose one, especially not like this. And, if there were any large-scale dealings going on, the bank must have known — though they'll never admit it."

Paul put more faith in Joe's efforts in locating Mirta, and indeed eventually someone told us, through Pepe, that he knew of a woman like that who felt she was bring hounded by the BA Police and had left town.

Patagonia, perhaps?

Dad said she favoured Patagonian rabbits.

Paul phoned The Divine Sibyl.

"Go East, not South," she said.

Of course, said Paul.

So Paul, Pepe, Joe and I set off in a rented Landrover taking the ferry across the River Plate to Colonia on the other side. On board we stayed close together to avoid a repetition of the reported loss of the red crocodile jacket last seen on Dad's back and later fished out of the river, the absurdly expensive leather slit with a stab wound.

Paul had of course been here before but we others were not prepared for the neat shabbiness of the Swiss colony we passed through on the road to Montevideo. Impoverished but clean, a community which had not lost its pride, a country that could go to the ballot-box and say a unanimous no to the death squads. However, in the splendid ruins of a once flourishing city my expectations were met with only more emptiness.

"We won't find anything here," said Paul, "let's head out towards Punta del Este!"

The highway going east was fairly quiet, old trucks trundling along, occasional buses, few long out-dated saloon cars, even a brave little Model T Ford, many bicycles. Our elderly Mendosa registered Landrover could count almost as a luxury vehicle, with a long wheelbase and its sideways benches in the back suggesting a personnel carrier.

"Probably ex-military," was Paul's opinion, and left it to me to drive. Pepe and Joe practiced jumping in and out under the rolled-up roof-flap without lowering the tailgate. They mostly talked about their shared passion for Westerns and war films.

Place names appeared on signposts along the way with no obvious settlements attached except maybe a bus-stop with lean-to shack selling fizzy drinks and cigarettes.

"The actual villages are off the highway, down on the coast," said Pepe.

We turned off every now and then through air scented with eucalyptus and dense clouds of mimosa blossom, roots doing their job of stabilising the shifting sands, avenues of lemons, small bungalows dotted among the trees; at the end a few shops where we'd buy a handful of sweets for the sake of asking questions, leaving it up to Pepe to go in and talk, not to be too obviously foreign. Pepe could say he was looking for his aunt to find out if there was a woman from Buenos Aires but any descriptions he was given were of families or couples that didn't tally. So we pressed on.

For Pepe and Joe it was as good as being in their own adventure film, with the same element of make-believe. Paul was quite relaxed about the whole thing, he wasn't expecting anything different from the last time. He was also too aware that it might be impossible to define success or failure even if we found what we were looking for.

"Any vibes coming through over the air-waves?" he asked me, keeping it light-hearted. "No messages from the Sibyl?"

Why did he ask me? He seemed to think I was the one in touch with the Other World. Was this to be my life, an endless quest based on guess-work, as when climbing the vast expanse of the Bernese Oberland in search of May? Frozen peaks of snow and granite or the flat delta of the River Plate, where I, a London boy, felt equally at a loss, disturbingly dislocated. I longed for Smiley or my Dad who could give me the inner strength he had in abundance. It wasn't only that my Dad loved me, he had that voice, unwavering eyes and those strong hands that assured me we were united against any misfortune life could throw at us. Maybe it was his voice I missed most of all.

As if he followed my thoughts Paul said:

"He used to talk endlessly on the phone. It never bothered him that we could be in opposite time zones, 3 o'clock in the morning London or lunchtime in Hong Kong made no difference, though I think on the whole he liked his audience to be lying comfortably in bed — certainly his women, or the men in their armchairs with a drink, it made them less fidgety. Husbands and wives used to complain when it went on for hours. But he didn't phone much from here, just a few words now and then usually to tell me something trivial like not to forget that the soft-shell crabs would be in season and his favourite beach-bar to eat them at. It didn't occur to him that we needed to know that he was safe and well."

I remembered being small enough to be carried around on his arm and his voice talking to me, and I had seen it again with the twins and their intense little faces as they stared at him trying to understand what he was telling them so seriously.

"So," said Paul, "at first I didn't even notice how long it had been since he called. It was Sibylla who was anxious about him. Even when I was in Boston and told her I had just spoken to him on the phone, the Sibyl was already sure of his death — though she could never say it out loud, as if the words would make it absolute. And so, unless you can believe that the sound got trapped in the ether and was released again after his death, either she was too anxious about him or I was too heedless of time passing."

"Atlantida," Pepe pointed to a signpost. "That's quite a big centre, a church and hotel. Let's stop and have something to eat in the hotel."

"In a café," said Paul. "No use going to a hotel, too transient."

We ate the usual slab of beef and went for a walk along the beach to stretch our legs. I began to feel more hopeful. This seemed like a real place at last, not a cardboard cut-out of a wild west town where nothing ever happens.

Something did happen here, I was sure of it.

Paul took over the driving and instead of turning back to the highway, he drove further along the coastal road through another small settlement. There, between Anna Castro's stall of calabazas and the butcher Portillo's display of carcasses, was an optimistic small estate agent's office offering to sell us a piece of The Earthly Paradise.

"Just the thing," said Paul and drew up outside. This time he went in himself and in his best upper-class Castellano asked about houses for sale or rent.

Answering Paul's questions, there were plenty of houses for rent, nearly all belonging to people from Buenos Aires. They liked it here for the quiet and simple life, the safety to let their children out to play, girls going dancing without being molested, so the Argentinos weren't selling their holiday homes even if at the moment they weren't coming to spend the summer. Selling would be a last act of desperation.

While the agent was talking, Paul was studying the map of the locality on the wall behind him, neatly dotted with little flags for the available properties in various colours, graded by cost.

"We share the same river, sea and sand, but we are better people. We may have poverty but we threw out the military and said no to the dollar. Argentines are shameless — and they've no manners."

He was quite prepared to take advantage of his foreign audience to vent his frustrations, and Paul let him rant on, until eventually he interrupted, saying:

"I'm trying to get to Mirta's house but I think I turned off too soon. Do I have to go back to main road to get there?"

"No," the agent said. "Everyone makes that mistake, that's why it's so hard to find. It's on this side of the arroyo. Just keep on until you can't go any further and you're there. She used to sell clams and razor-shells but I'm not sure she does any more. The oil drums rusted through and they are hard to replace."

"How did you know?" I asked as soon as we were back in the Landrover.

"The map. The houses became fewer and cheaper the further east from here, but approaching from the highway they were much more expensive. That last phone call — he mentioned Mirta and her summer cabin on the Solis Chico... I didn't remember until I saw it on the map."

A Paradise on Earth, the estate agent promised.

I felt sick with anticipation. I could almost feel his presence.

As we drove on beyond the centre, fewer houses, mostly either unfinished or already in ruins, a tomorrow and a yesterday, but no today. But nearing the fresh water of the *arroyo* the vegetation was richer, eucalyptus gave way to oleanders, pink flowers enticing the shimmering excitement of hummingbirds...

... how many hummingbirds does it take to change the course of history, how many rusty oil drums of razor shell clams Mirta might sell for a peso a dozen, to tip the balance?

... then, where even the Landrover dared venture no further, in a hollow in the dunes under a windbreak of acacias, a solitary shack with shirts on a line... I knew it immediately, I'd recognise those shirts anywhere, threadbare as they were, faded Swiss cotton...

"Dad, Dad, it's Con..."

For a second I thought I saw a man emerge, slightly stooped through the low door, with long fading red hair — but this was the Sibyl's image, not mine. What I saw was a middle-aged woman, sturdy, square face, dressed in a man's shirt and trousers, defiant, defensive.

"It took you a long time to get here," she said in *castellano platensis*.

"The last time I tried," said Paul, "I couldn't find you. People said you'd gone away."

"I went but I couldn't stay away," she said. "When I came back my house had been destroyed so I built this here out of the wreckage. I look out to sea and think he'll come up over the dune the way he used to after his swim, as if I hadn't seen him with my own eyes in the sand with a bullet-hole in the back of his head. When I turned him over he was smiling at me in a happy dream."

For years I had believed that he was dead, telling myself that he wasn't coming back — ever. But now I couldn't believe it any more. Words were too weak to convince me. Even when she went on telling what to her were the facts — I couldn't accept them.

"I dug a shallow hole under the bushes to hide him but when I came back three days later with the men from the *Banco Suizo Unido* he was gone. I don't know if they believed me or not but they took me in their car back to Buenos Aires. But I didn't feel safe so I took the Patagonian Express south out of harm's way for a bit."

Every word she said I imprinted in my memory so I could repeat it for the Divine Sibyl to check it against her version, to see if she believed that's what had really happened. Maybe the Sibyl knew even more than Mirta.

"Who shot him?" Paul asked.

Mirta shrugged.

"They were all the same to me. In BA they accused him of selling guns to the subversives. He didn't deny or confirm this, merely said one could get guns anywhere as long as one had dollars. Maybe he was supplying the dollars for them, I don't know. What worried me was that I really didn't know, so if they tortured me I'd have had nothing to tell. And no way to save myself."

She spoke as if this were a well-known fact, but for me, coming from Geneva, I could hardly believe that this was possible. I looked to Paul for his reaction but clearly it was nothing strange to him. He had heard it before.

"So I brought him here to get away from it all, my secret place, *el Paraiso del Mundo* as they call it on the billboards. Oh, Dear Mother of God, but he was a man to die for!"

Dad used to say that Luck was really Chaos, which started with the Big Bang, following its own internal logic to the bitter end. At what point in an eternity of chaos had this woman been designated as his Lady Luck?

"But he was a terrible fidget," she said, "he just couldn't keep quiet, or even try to stay out of trouble. The next thing, he was fixing guns for a gang from Montevideo who came out here to lie low as well. He was in the yard using wine bottles for target practice when Carlos Suarez, the poet, turned up and when he saw that their stash of guns had been discovered under the heap of bottles they argued amongst themselves about the need to shoot him, so he bargained with them that he'd be their gunsmith as long as they didn't expect him to get involved in their quarrels. Dear Lord, but they'd sit here all night watching him at work — he knew his business all right — yes, of course, he said, he trained in the Swiss army, the best in the world — and debating tactics. He'd tell them what they'd done wrong. He knew everything: from how to equip and mobilise an army to how to negotiate a cease-fire — unless you've won, he said, you don't, you fight to the last man. He blamed them for fools when he realised they were involved in the kidnap of that AID agent. The whole country was paralysed while the search for him was on until they found his body in a house in Carrasco. So a squad came out looking for the killers. Unperturbed, he went for his usual dip in the ocean · he'd swim out and play around with the dolphins — just when they came beating this way through the trees — I couldn't warn him but he must have been aware because he stood a while naked on the shoreline as if counting the waves, waiting for the seventh, then pulled on his trousers and walked away slowly in the opposite direction, away from me. I was terrified for him and for myself. I heard a shot but didn't dare go out to look until first light in the morning."

Not a bad-looking woman, wearing his shirts, not young, not beautiful — my glorious Dad who had my lovely mother and the Divine Sibyl, perhaps even the magnificent Mrs Hein to love him, smiling in death at a common woman he picked up at the race course in Palermo!

Why?

Why? I asked the Divine Sibyl.

"We all believed he was smiling for us," she said. "He was Love Itself."

I went to visit May somewhere in South Africa, not because the Sibyl had asked me to go but because May sent me a message that she needed to see me. I had no wish to see her, to tell her that the man who had picked us up by a hand each to stop us fighting was last seen dead on the remotest shore of the River Plate.

Following May's instructions, after arrival at International I was dropped off by car at some obscure airstrip where I sat on my back-pack, and waited. My state of mind was such that I could have been sitting there a week later and hardly have noticed it — though I suppose hunger would have driven me to make a move. The red earth and spindly trees scarcely made any impact on my senses and there was little activity around the three or four Fokker-type aircraft parked alongside. So I had no idea of how long I'd been there before a single turbo-prop landed and taxied to where I was sitting.

"Jump up" said Roger from the open door and gave me a hand, and we took off again with hardly a pause. There were two European couples sitting behind enjoying the adventure and crying out with excitement at every animal they saw in the scarcely changing landscape below. When one of the women offered to make room for me among the paying passengers Roger gestured to me to stay where I was, squatting beside him.

"Is he your brother?" one of them asked me.

"He could be," I answered, laughing it off.

Accepting that I was to be the crew, I helped unload the four passengers with their luggage, and some crates of groceries, fruit and drink at a safari lodge in the middle of nowhere. Not having eaten any of the airline food offering, I was tempted by the shady lodge veranda with tables laid out for the new arrivals but apart from handing me a water bottle, Roger allowed no time for refreshment.

"Home before sunset," was all he said so I sat and admired his skill and confidence in the cockpit — just like my Dad. Dad hated khaki shorts — unSwiss — but Roger looked good in them. His darkly dynamic mother had at least saved him from the curse of pink skin and freckles though he had ginger hair on his legs and a fuzz of gold on his arms from elbow to the knuckles of his hands. I had completely missed out on my Dad's most distinguishing feature. I was surprised to notice the pilot's left hand was wearing a signet ring on the little finger, it seemed out of character in Roger who was embarrassed by any form of ostentation.

"What's the ring?" I asked.

He held it out to me: an onyx disk with the intaglio carving of a tiny skull, the seal of a death-head. I recognised it.

"How did you get it?"

"Smiley."

"I didn't know you had it. You never wore it before," I remarked.

"I can't at home, my mother tries to get it off me, she seems to think she should have it. Now of course it's May who thinks it's rightfully hers, that she could use it as a Totenkopf seal, probably what Smiley used it for."

I too was envious, but Roger wasn't going to give away his one Smiley memento.

May came running out of a house or hut — all the architecture had the temporary air of being thrown up in a hurry, except for one larger house at a distance, Dutch Colonial, I presumed — and she waited impatiently for me to get down so she could hug me. Gratified at this enthusiastic reception I hugged her back, and then disgraced myself by weeping over her shoulder. I was forced at last to say what I refused to believe, that my father was not only dead, but lost without a trace.

"Darling Connie," she said, holding on to me and leading me to her house. "You're a hero."

I shook my head, too distressed to speak.

We were joined by an older woman from the proper brick house, who was introduced as Maddie of the *Ethnic Lekkerbekken*. She too hugged me and in an almost precise repetition of Mrs Hein's greeting she said:

"So you're the angelic wife's boy! Fortunate young man, the legitimate son and heir."

A hearty, generous woman, she disconcerted me even more than Mrs Hein did.

They sat me down with mealy crackers, quite normal cheese and a bottle of good wine and gathered around looking at me expectantly.

What could I say? Facing them my sense of failure became even more overwhelming.

"What do you want me to say?" I cried. "That my amazingly marvellous, wonderful father spent the last months of his life with a whore playing dirty war games with a gang of South American thugs? I can't and I won't."

"I should have been so lucky!" said Maddie, and blundered her way out the door, back to her Afrikaner stronghold.

We three.

"We have one another," said May.

I assumed that by now Roger had been roped in as sex partner just as I had been, but like me he wasn't her lover.

Then May announced the purpose of her summons: "I've something to give you."

Rolled up into a small bundle was a pair of Hermès chinos: bleached almost white, well worn but clean; a watch: Jaeger le Coultre, apparently undamaged but stopped at 9:23 — no complications and so no date; and, in a waterproof zip-lock envelope, the red of a Swiss passport.

I knew instantly what this little bundle represented. The three last things of a man's life.

"Where did you get it?" I asked.

"It was delivered by post to *Totenkopf (Schweiz)* in Bern," said May. "Grimsi sent it on to me with a box of bullets for the SIG 210. He worries that I may run out of ammunition — I don't know what he imagines I do all day here apart from shooting the natives — or lions."

"The more significant thing is, where was it sent from?" I said.

"Postmark Bern. Some federal office. Grimsi asked but they said that as far as they knew it came in by diplomatic bag, presumably someone's lost property."

From that I had to conclude that Ueli Mueller was doing his job. So I told them about my visit to Buenos Aires, without too many details, but at the end:

"I failed to get a body to bring home to Mum. It just wasn't there. She's disappointed, so now I wish I'd left her as she was, resigned, without expectations."

"You're a hero for trying and you came home with a story."

"An inconclusive one. One woman saw him dead, and covered the body with sand to hide it. Three days later it wasn't there. It sounds remarkably like a resurrection to me."

Walking that empty strand I had refused to discuss the event with Paul or Joe, and certainly not Pepe or Mr Mueller. I didn't want their opinions disturbing the vision I was struggling to form in my own mind of what really happened.

So when my support team was getting ready to go home I had said: "I'm not coming with you. I've not finished here."

"I understand you don't want to give up," said Paul, "but don't lose your sense of proportion. Remember, your mother bravely survived the loss of your father, but losing you would be a disaster."

With Mirta I had no axe to grind, the roll of dollars she had hidden in her shack was sufficient for her needs so she could go on living with the undying vision of him reappearing up over the dunes any day now.

I shook out the chinos and held them up against me. They'd be a good fit except a little short in the leg, easily rectified. I draped them over the back of a chair. I polished up the Jaeger le Coultre with my handkerchief and tested the spring. It wound up quite well though obviously it could do with proper cleaning and lubrication. I put it on my wrist, replacing the cheap but sturdy Mondaine railway watch I'd favoured since my first days in Geneva. Then I opened the envelope and extracted the passport. I knew what I possessed.

"Mine," I said, and put it in my pocket.

Not bone, flesh or blood, but the next best thing: inseparable in life, more durable in death. 99.9% of the man; I should be content, and cherish the 0.01% uncertainty left to spice my life, my vision of him walking in the door and asking what I was doing, sitting at his desk.

"Thank you for passing it on, May. You could have just kept it as a souvenir. Or Roger for that matter,"

"Well, you heard what Maddie said," said Roger. "The legitimate son and heir. I've got Dadi Hein."

"And I've got Grimsi," said May. "Not that he makes up for the loss of my Daddy — but you have no one else."

"I have his name and his office. I'll follow on where he left off."

But May was right, more than anything we had one another. So I could tell them what the Sibyl told me not to tell Goosie who was not, after all, one of We Three.

"Your father didn't deliberately keep secrets from your mother," the Sibyl said, "but neither did he tell her things she didn't need to know — and she didn't ask. She trusted him not to jeopardise their marriage. I'm not advising you one way or the other, I'm just telling you that you have to use your judgement and act responsibly — like your father."

"I stayed on with Mirta after the Landrover with the others left for the journey back," I told them. "Day after day I walked up and down that expanse of beach trying to think myself into what it would be like to know someone is lurking in the scrub behind the dunes with a gun and my head as its target. And what then? Mirta said she buried him, but in that soft, shifting sand she wouldn't have been able to dig deep and if she covered his face with her scarf — or if his fellow conspirators came looking for their gunsmith — or the possibility I began to see now, in the light of the salvaged trousers and passport, was that a Swiss recovery party could have come ahead of Mirta with the official one to remove all traces of their countryman and protect his secrets — possibly even now, acting according to their principles, he was neatly buried in some Swiss cemetery and his possessions duly returned to his heir. It may well have taken that long for them finally to identify him as *Totenkopf (Schweiz) GmbH* in the *Kügelgassli*, the millwheel of Swiss bureaucracy grinding on as usual slowly, slowly — Grimsi might even have had it tucked away in a cubbyhole for a while without it occurring to him to do anything about it. He was employed to answer the phone, write out orders and keep the accounts, which he had done faithfully, awaiting further instructions.

At the time that I was exploring the beach this last possibility was unknown, so as there was nothing for me to find on that wind-swept stretch of sand, there where the waters pouring down from the Paranà, the Iguazù and the Uruguay meet and mingle with the South Atlantic.

Every *tardecer*, the time of day when late afternoon quickens into dusk, I'd wander back to Mirta and sit watching her at her wood-burning stove preparing the evening soup of potatoes, carrots and onion, spiced up with whatever else was available, leaves of chard or some chicken wings — she would send me out to drag in a length of tree-trunk, which, propped up at the mouth of the stove, shortened into ash as it was slowly consumed by the fire, Mirta standing by in an attitude of patient contentment, stirring the sad remnants of the day into the blackened old cast-iron pot.

Leaving the pot half off the ring to simmer, she'd lean back against the wall. She timed her cooking by the length of a cigarette, supporting her bosom on her folded arm as she smoked. Dad didn't smoke, he gave it up aged 17 — previously he and Joey had rolled illicit cigarillos with the leaves smuggled in by Joey from his father's tobacco farm on the Limpopo, but never after...

I could never eat soup like that again. Even the smell evoked Mirta and her method of cutting bread. It alarmed me, how she held the loaf against her breast, I could hardly restrain myself from snatching the knife away from her...

Dad must have observed the same ritual many times and I wondered what he saw when he looked at her: her hunched-up shoulders relaxing, tight waist and solid mare-like haunches letting go, succumbing to the quiet of the night. Did the spark of desire come from seeing her like this or was he just happy to have a brief respite of peace in her company?

While I lay sleepless on the sofa I thought of him in the inner room with this woman. He must have been good with her to have gained such loyalty and bitter regret. If that bullet hadn't stopped him dead in his tracks he could have carried on here in a Robinson Crusoe existence indefinitely. So could I, I could stay and live out his life for him... it was time I left! But when I told Mirta I was going back to Buenos Aires to catch my flight home she said she'd come with me. She too had unfinished business.

"I've crossed this water so often," she said. "Always with a certain trepidation. The best time was also the worst, with *tu Papa*. He'd engaged me to do his laundry — though he always complained I didn't do his shirts properly — so when he talked himself out of the slaughterhouse he made his way to me to rest up and recover — they'd been careful not to leave any obvious bruises — oddly enough pain seemed to stimulate him; the release of hormones, he said, gave him relief. Such an intelligent, well-spoken man, yet at times he seemed to talk nonsense. He said he was expecting to meet his friend Joey soon, but when I asked who Joey was he said: just a boy I knew at school. We were best friends until I shot him."

Why? This was the one utterly taboo subject at home yet here he was mentioning it casually to a strange woman, as if Joey were alive and well and coming to meet him on the Solis Chico.

I stood looking at the wake of foam from under the hydrofoil leaving Uruguay and its unsolved riddle behind. Before I came here I had an image of what I might find, a decayed corpse, a skeleton in pieces maybe. Now I had nothing.

With Mirta beside me, I could feel myself becoming a different person, or maybe not so much different but, stepping into my ballsy Dad's footprints, the grown-up version of me. We walked across the gangplank onto the quay towards the motley confusion of taxis and cabs, then paused with our bags at our feet. I asked where she was going, hesitating about the propriety of inviting her to come back to my hotel with me. *The Four Seasons* was a bit up-market for Mirta though now that she was wearing a flowery dress that showed her shapely ankles and plump calves under a short coat, and had combed out the tangly curls that framed her face, she had turned herself into quite an attractive woman. The sharp twitchy sensation growing more urgent down below acknowledged that.

"Home," she said, surprised I asked. "My aunt and I share a yard, she has one side and I the other. I think you'd like to come home with me."

Not conceding either a yes or a no I picked up her small suitcase and followed her across the quay.

We entered Mirta's place by an archway in a row of tall townhouses and I could see the point of having an Aunt Julia in residence, there to repel squatters in the form of relatives up from the country, from taking over what was a very desirable little residence in the heart of the city — perhaps the local equivalent of a London mews. Sheltered by the walls of the surrounding buildings, in the small yard the city noise was reduced to a quiet hum and it felt completely private. I could picture my Dad keeping his pale skin and freckles in the shade of the central fig tree while his shirts and underpants dried in the sun, entertaining Mirta and being entertained in his turn by tall tales from their unconventional lives. This beginning to my affairs would be the continuation of hers. I had a lot to live up to.

Act responsibly, said the Sibyl. Like your father.

Typically cryptic Sibylline advice!

As I told my story, May and Roger watched me intently. We were in it together. What one did affected the other two and I had brought a Mirta into their lives just as May had brought a Grimsi into ours. Probably they would never meet, but she was there nevertheless as part of me.

I had acted responsibly, just like our fathers.

"What was it like?" asked May, knowing my only previous experience was with her.

"Dark," I said. "A lovely dark chocolaty pool of sensation to sink into and drown."

"Oh..." said May, knowing she'd never achieve that degree of melting tenderness to make men sigh with that kind of rapture.

"When I told the Divine Sibyl what her rival was like she just nodded as if she already knew and wasn't a bit put out. Melting chocolate is richly satisfying but it isn't divine. Besides, though she says she suffers terribly from jealousy, she was honestly just happy that he'd had that final pleasure."

It wasn't my experience she was curious about, but Dad's.

"Mama isn't a bit jealous," said May. "She has no reason to be."

"Mirta says I fuck like my father," I said, blushing but unable to resist passing on that glorious accolade — so much for being a responsible adult!

"So you should," said May. "You spied on him often enough. And if it's true then I know how he fucked as well because I know you. And I can pass it on to Roger. We three."

May hugged us both. I hoped she wouldn't be jealous that, charismatic person as she was, her sister was the girl I was already adoring to the end of my days, like Dad adored our lovely and divine mothers.

With May and Roger's sympathy not belittling my futile effort, I began to feel less devastated by my South American venture. Alongside the bitter disappointment of not finding my Dad, I hadn't known how to tell them about the affair with Mirta. But they hadn't laughed at her either, so I could admit my true feeling of gratitude for the amazing revelation she gave me into my Dad's use of love to give him courage and consolation.

I hoped that Roger, who had *Hein Precision Instruments* behind him, wouldn't resent me that I was indeed the legitimate son and heir. It might even be true that power rests in the size of one's penis. My Dad was never intimidated because he could work out the pecking order from observations in the locker rooms at both home and away games. That was one useful kind of knowledge he acquired in the four and a half years he said he wasted by having to go to school. The pre-school training in mental arithmetic he got from his grandfather Conrad, seeing the size, shape and weight of numbers, was the real basis of his fortune. Like me, his fluency in the regional vari- ations of Swiss and Afrikaans was insignificant. Language is in the air around one, one has only to listen, the lively little synapses in the brain make the connections to do the rest.

"We three can run linked enterprises," said Roger. "You in London, May in Bern and me here, that covers the useful part of the world, where Swiss-ness applies. The rest is just there for trade. We will keep the *Totenkopf* alive and thriving."

"You'd better add gun-smithing to your engineering and flying skills," said May. "Then like my Daddy you can pass your idle hours with a file and greasy rag. That'll keep Grimsi happy and the income steady. Diamonds and gold is the fluctuating fancy stuff, good to gamble with, guns are dependable."

"That leaves me the really serious stuff," I said, "the pharmaceuticals."

"About which," said May," "you know absolutely nothing."

"I don't need to. Dipping randomly into tapes of Dad's conversations, I discovered someone called Schletti..."

"Your Grimsi!" said May, delighted.

"I'm arranging with him to help me move the fungus production out of China into a suitably swampy bit of Mexico, well away from prying gringos. At least I can speak the language. I remember Dad describing his little borrowed bit of China as quaintly folkloresy with experimental frogs croaking around on rafts of algae. But as the Chinese situation can blow up any minute when they take back Hong Kong and I have no death-wish... Mum says it was hard enough maintaining the frog population back then, when she and her lady friends ran a frog protection society — I don't know if they realised they were being used as a cover for the drug extraction — when we leave, the locals will eat the frogs and be poisoned by the fungi. So there won't be any copycat pro-duction left behind to spoil our reputation and our profits."

"It will be quite an undertaking to move the essentials," said Roger. "I'll be your confidential pilot. The Pilatus isn't quite long-haul enough so I'd better start looking around to lease an aircraft that's more suitable."

Roger was reluctantly pleased to have an excuse to fly bigger, maybe something with a nice Rolls Royce engine.

We were re-shaping our inheritance to fit our own size, shape and desires.

The race was also on which of we three would make the most of the dif-ferent legacies our father left us.

"We three together," said May, "can make up for one of him."

"Dad's suits need only a tiny alteration to fit me," I said, thinking myself into my role as the financial genius of we three — not that May would concede me that title. "The jackets are fine, the trousers were a little tight in the bum, but when the centre seam is let out they hang longer in the leg. He was pernickety about having a tight crotch to hold in his bulgy balls."

As a six-year-old I had boasted that I could read and write better than Our Father of the Almighty Balls. He explained his were like that because they were symmetrical so they sat balanced equally up-front. Mine happily dangled down more modestly out of the way leaving it up to Cock to declare his presence, which he was doing quite satisfactorily.

"All I want," I said, "is snug without exaggeration."

May laughed at me.

"Now you're talking just like him — as if all the boss needs to impress the workers is a superbly fitting suit with a fine genital display..."

"That's not how it works," I explained. "The suit gives me confidence and the boss's confidence overawes the staff — as well as him being obviously right."

I had travelled in a summer-weight light grey suit with a fine blue and white striped shirt, still wearing what I had chosen for flying to South America. Obviously it was having the desired effect because Maddie phoned across to invite me to have supper and find a comfortable bed with her.

Oh, for pity's sake, I thought, will all my Dad's old loves expect me to step into his shoes? Or are they just curious?

But then, so was I. Just curious.

What I liked about Maddie's house was that dead animals were confined to the kitchen as food. There was no use of heads, horns or skins as décor. After Mirta, it was Maddie's turn to have me sitting at her kitchen table. Watching her prepare an ostrich egg omelette with chunks of something that might have been bacon — or maybe not — I was startled to see the mother ostrich staring in through the window. Beyond her were about 50 more crowding in to have a look at the stranger.

"Before Roger came here with his transport business the birds had a much freer life. Now I have to keep them away from his runways. I'm not that sure I really like Roger. A fine young man, he has the attractively straight-faced looks all right but with that uncompromising earnest manner he's too Swiss."

I too was getting that long-jawed look as I lost the cheerful boy face, but I'd never be as über-cool as Roger.

"He insists I stick rigidly to the recipes of the stuff I sell," Maddie explained. "He's complains that by including anything too fanciful on the spur of the moment I could make people sick and ruin his reputation, or get him into trouble about export licences. But all people really want to buy is my hot chilli paste, I sell 100 jars to one chocolate-crusted locust. It's my best effort, what I used to castrate your Dad so he couldn't perform on his wedding night. Little wonder your mother hates me — don't worry, I wouldn't dream of using it on you even as a stimulant. I'll have you *au naturel,* the way your Dad preferred it."

When Dad told his funny stories about his adventures with women, my childish imagination never grasped the reality behind them, but this was clearly one of them — an Afrikaner lady with a chancy line in ethnic foods who excited his love of risk-taking. I could feel my balls burning already. I could hardly wait to get in there and quench the fire.

"Honey-bee ice-cream," she said, offering me a gourd-shaped dish with a horn spoon. The ice-cream was pale with beads of honey mixed in but also what looked like actual bits of bee, legs and wings.

"It's perfectly safe," she said, seeing my hesitation. "Only be careful that there might be a sting that got in by mistake. Most of my students are painfully conscientious but some can be a bit lackadaisical. Just spit it out if you come across any. Your Dad really loved my puff-adder stew with roasted ground-nuts. The adders are hard to catch but I always kept a few in the freezer for him and when he was here he'd make day-long trips, going out to find more for me."

I was glad to hear that Roger was exercising some quality control.

My Dad gave lectures on business ethics but I could see that for himself he was cursed with the Joey syndrome of dicing with death.

She babbled on about her outlandish recipes while I cautiously worked my way through her honey bees. It was an intriguing mixture of sharply sweet with an occasional crunch of bitterness. The extraordinary thing was that the sweet was so enticing one risked the sting for the adventure of the next bite.

But I resolved to escape before having to face the test of the puff-adders.

As the pitch-black night grew cold Maddie heaped up a fire of spiny brush and roots on the hearth and invited me to lie down beside her naked body basking in its glow on the thick hand-knotted hearth-rug. A lioness, I was captivated by her figure, her presence as a tawny blond African, caught in a kind of timeless, ageless prime of life — why did she live here alone with her house, her students, her research station? Because, it was implied, she fell in love with my father when as youngsters they met at her brother's funeral and though he came to visit her bringing, as the beeps and whirr- ings of his machines revealed to me, arms-embargo breaking guns, and tak- ing out equally illegal diamonds, he would never stay long.

Of course not, he had my darling mum to come home to.

Maddie hated my mother while Mum merely disapproved of her — not that Mum ever forgave her for the incident with the chilli paste, though whenever she and the Divine discussed it, it sent the Divine into fits of giggles as if at a huge joke and Mum smiled indulgently in retrospect at Dad's peccadillos. Neither did she forgive the mad Afrikaanse for fiddling with the bridegroom's fly-buttons at the wedding banquet, bringing it to an abrupt end when the guests nearest and dearest to him rose up around him in a flap, the headmaster's wife — she of the chocolate éclairs — asking plaintively what was going on and Grandfather trying to make her look the other way.

So lying with her in the starry black African night was a way of finding out why. And whether the sex was worth the risk.

It was like eating honey-bee ice-cream.

And the very fact of surviving her praying mantis embrace gave me not only the satisfaction of great sex but tremendous mental strength as well. I could feel myself acutely self-aware to the tips of my extremities. Women! Mirta had had it too, that ageless quality. As had Mum and the Sibyl. With my body I worshipped them all and I sang with happiness at having a life so full of riches.

I checked how well Dad's watch was keeping time after its wanderings in the unknown — it had lost three minutes since I wound it yesterday, but I'd have it fixed when I got back to its birthplace near Geneva when I went to collect my diplomas, awards and prizes — and I put on his chinos. They were worn to the shape of his body and I had the sensation of becoming one with him with them on. I'd bought a pair of high-top desert boots in Weinberg's before coming to Africa so the slightly shorter leg didn't matter and a few more nights with the likes of mad Maddie would soon have me filling out the bulges. But I was resolved to eat no more *Lekkerbekken* and strolled across to May for breakfast.

She and Roger were discussing the day's schedule.

"You can come and crew for me again, *broerke*," said Roger, making a joke of his passenger's question yesterday.

"I'd rather you lent me a bed to lie down in," I said. "I haven't been sleeping much lately and your Maddie drained me dry last night. A fantastic woman, have you... ?"

"Are you crazy?" said Roger. "She'd eat me alive... "

"The Sibyl says your mother is worried you might marry May. Why, when you know you can't?"

"Marriage as in a legal contract to live together with shared responsibilities. That would suit me fine."

"And sex..."

"We don't need a piece of paper for that. Any more than you do."

I turned to May who was keeping aloof from man-talk.

"Would Grimsi approve of *Totenkopf (Schweiz)* marrying the *Smiley Bush Pilot Enterprise*?"

"Grimsi is my partner. I'm not marrying anyone just now, and certainly not Roger, that bossy-cock with red hair! I'd be mad. And a Jewish Mother into the bargain — how did you avoid getting the snip?" she asked Roger.

"Dadi Hein said it's because I was a defenceless infant, and they should wait till I had some say in the matter. Smiley said don't, there's no point in mutilating oneself in the name of hygiene. We're not in the desert, we have the facilities to wash properly. But that was only to annoy Grandfather Bott with whom he was in relentless opposition over everything — except for the diamonds. Opi misses having his pick of the the best gems and he actually quite misses the rows and arguments too. He says Smiley was worth having a fight with. He has given up going to shul because he can't rail at Yahweh any more, not as long as He is blessing him with a peaceful and prosperous old age. Besides, he has to admit that granting him the privilege of killing Nazis when he was with the Eighth Army was a satisfactory small recompense for His past failings."

"I need to get back to Grimsi," said May. "I've instructed him that if any of Daddy's old hunting rifles come up for sale to buy them back. Grimsi and Mr Mug are working on it. Mr Mug knows the original buyers so he is good at hunting them down."

Grimsi and Mr Mug! A formidable pair of twisters in the esoteric world of rare guns.

"They should be mine," I protested. "Dad made them in the London workplace."

"Less than half," said May, "and the skill came from SIG and shooting contests when he was in Bern. But I'll do a deal with you, I've a nice one from Düsseldorf with a boar's head on the reverse of the Totenkopf, dated 1978. I'll swop that for his old Armee Sturmgewehr."

"I don't know where it is," I said, feeling foolish. It had never occurred to me to look for it. The press in his study was empty. Mum didn't like him keeping guns in the house.

"I suppose it's where it always was," said May. "In the boot of the Jaguar, that was his real gun press."

Perhaps.

Uncle Toby, Dad's solicitor, was a Quaker and sensitive about such things so May was probably right that if he knew it was locked up in the boot he'd leave it there untouched. He and Aunt Amanda were really only Willie's aunt and uncle, however Toby was Dad's study-mate from school so that made him our honorary uncle too. When he sold Dad's riverside apartment they took the Jaguar to their house in Dorset where there was enough old barn to store any number of cars. I would get Willie on my side to go down on a visit. Willie would find the key — he was that kind of boy — and we'd have a root around under the bales of hay Aunt Amanda's horse munched her way through every winter. We'd have to have something like a cricket bag to smuggle it out in.

Leaving it up to me to pursue my claim to the guns as best I could, May asked:

"Now you've survived one night with the preying mantis are you staying on for more?"

I thought of the stomach-churning stew that might be on the menu next and said I'd be leaving as soon as possible. If Roger would drop me off in Johannesburg on the day's safari, I could get the next flight to Zürich.

"And leave me here alone at the mercy of the Mad Madigan!" said Roger, acting dismayed. But I knew perfectly well that he was more than a bit envious of his *broerke's* exploits in the sex arena and intrigued by where an affair with the man-muncher might lead him.

"Be careful," I said. "If she takes a fancy to you, you may not survive."

"And stick to the baked aardvark," said May, "don't be tempted to try experiments with any aphrodisiac — her students are always making themselves sick convinced they'll make a fortune if they can only hit on the right bug or creepy-crawly. My Daddy said success isn't luck, it comes by taking your work seriously, not by larking about and hoping to get lucky."

"Honey-bee ice-cream seems to work," I said. "If you get a chance you can save a sample and send it to me to have analysed — I can get Schletti working on it and it can go into production along with the swampy frog fungus."

My *Swampy Frog Fungus* eventually proved the most profitable of my ventures, a solid basis on which to build all the others.

Since I had to leave Dad's watch behind in the rue du Rhone to be fixed, I looked around for a temporary replacement and immediately did the Swiss thing and chose the most irresistibly beautiful, technically perfect Patek Phillipe timekeeper, my ironic tribute of the Calvinist edict against the vanity of jewels. My Dad would approve. As it happened I didn't go back to Geneva for many years, it was Roger who collected the Jaeger-le Coultre and kept it. It was Papi Hein who had given it to Dad in the first place so, along with the death's head signet ring, the Hein possessions were returning to where they belonged.

Then, after I'd shaken hands with my professors and received the paper, gold and silver evidence of my two year stint being educated to the highest standard of European civilisation, I travelled back to London with Pepe.

Pepe was still convinced he was my best friend and because I casually mentioned that doing a course at LSE might be a shortcut to understanding my place in the global economy, he decided that's where he would study too. So, almost unintentionally, I added a degree in economics to my collection of fairly useless paper achievements. As maverick Dad had done all right without any but I was entering a different world.

Pepe was enthusiastic when the new Macintosh computer joined the array on Dad's desk. He wanted more than anything to sit there and play with it all day, and I got used to him being part of my office in addition to the furniture.

A breakthrough in unlocking the secrets of the winks and beeps came when I found myself quite unexpectedly talking to Grimsi.

"What do you want?" he asked and I could almost see him opening his gun drawer. Would he shoot at my voice?

"To talk to May," I said, not betraying my surprise.

"*Nei!*" he said. "Gone away."

I didn't believe him but the connection was broken off. I spent the rest of the day trying to work out how that had happened. Pepe's opinion was that somehow the Bern end had left a line open. Grimsi was probably equally shocked when he realised I could hear him talking. I tried to recall Dad's hand movements when he was sitting in my chair but all I could remember was that like a crocodile he smiled only when he was being wicked, but from the way his eyes crinkled up when he looked down at me building lines of dominos across the floor I knew that inside he was really smiling at me.

Mum used to complain that when Dad was abroad, in Hong Kong maybe or America, all she ever got on the phone was his secretary who would offer to pass on a message, look you. Sometimes he phoned back straight away or else it might be days later. No one ever seemed to know for sure where he was. So now the same thing was happening with May. Not long after Grimsi said she had gone away she phoned back herself full of enthusiasm to report that she had been visiting an African chief, "doing business:"

"Is that wise?" I asked, horrified. Grimsi was bad enough but at least he was safely Swiss, not a black African.

"Don't be silly, Con!" said May. "He's our best client. He told me that he and my Daddy were the worst boys in the school, condemned to sit together at the back of the class. He had to pinch Daddy to make him wake up and paid him £5 an essay to dictate it to him. He passed all his exams with top marks though Daddy never passed an exam in his life because he was dyslexic and no one taught him to read and write properly."

"My Dad could write," I said, "only no one could read it because he learned by watching his grandfather Conrad write in Russian so the letters were all the wrong shape. I tried to teach him how to do it right but he said he couldn't be bothered to learn when he had me to be his scribe. I thought that's what I'd be doing when I grew up."

"But anyway," said May, as usual ignoring my contrary version, "they made heaps of money together so it didn't matter. You should see Grimsi's face when they talk on the phone, he doesn't like big black men. That is why

I went to see him in person. He treated me like the Queen and said I am worthy of my father's Great White Spirit. I think he was being sarcastic."

I was annoyed as well as feeling quite sick with envy.

"Maddie is furious I didn't take her with me when I told her about the feasts we had, mostly zebu and goat, and as delicacy, filet of crocodile. Truly, truly, truly revolting! She'd have loved it."

As usual May was refusing to acknowledge the reality of my Dad as if only hers had a valid existence. Relationships were easier to understand when her Mama and my Dad were lovers. Uncle Gus, who at that time was very young and incredibly good-looking and clever, and would be a lordly Baron and Peer of the Realm when his Ancient Ancestors died off, only smiled tolerantly and said :

"I am the long-distance runner."

How right he was! He married the Divine Sibyl knowing what he was letting himself in for. It was worth it.

May was doing what I so badly wanted, and succeeding with envious ease with her Grimsi at her side.

But by now I was getting my own team together.

"What happened to Dad's secretary?" I asked Mum.

"The tiresome Gladys?" said Mum.

'Where is she now?"

"I suppose where she always was: a voice on the phone saying he's away, for sure, but she'd pass on the message — only now even she can't reach him with her messages."

When at last I did decipher her name on a phone line I was not a bit surprised that it led me back to Basel. When I asked Schletti if he knew her he said, "Of course! She was always at the other end of the boss's line."

Another possible to add to my team.

"Would you like to take a trip down to see the Sibyl?" I asked Mum.

"Whenever you like, dearest," she said and promptly cancelled her other arrangements.

Darling Mum, prepared to drop everything for the pleasure of an expedition with me!

We went in her hatchback Peugeot which was fitted out for transporting her falcons to their flights on the downs.

"Why don't you get yourself a car?" she asked.

"I don't need one," I said.

Though, thinking of the Jaguar mouldering away quietly at Uncle Toby's, I remarked:

"Anyway, where would I put it?"

Her car took the designated resident's space on the square formerly occupied by Dad's Jaguar. Madge's was stabled nearby in a rented mews. Paul didn't keep one of his own, taking taxis or borrowing a foreign office one for longer journeys. Pepe had an old Fiat he kept at the Argie hostel where he lived with his fellow anarchists. I wasn't keen on travelling with Pepe as his driving was also a bit too anarchic. When he got hooted at I had to remind him that London isn't Buenos Aires.

"I suppose not deciding to have a car reflects the uncertainty of my future."

"You've all the time in the world," said Mum.

She accepted Pepe was my nice college chum who always stopped by to say good morning to her when he came to the house, just as being a student at a reputable place of learning was occupation enough for me and justified postponing any decision about my future. I didn't want to worry her by mentioning Schletti and the resurgence of frogs.

With the amount of money Mum had flowing into her bank account every quarter without her ever having to think about it, she had lost touch with the necessity of actually doing anything to earn it. But then, she never had. When she got engaged to Dad she was eighteen, he was twenty-eight and doing well with his workshop off the Westway producing specialised medical instruments. All that was ever expected of her was to look beautiful wearing couture and high-end jewellery at City functions and produce a few sons to make sense of a big house in Bayswater —

at least that is what one would give as a rational explanation for their successful marriage.

In fact of course, it was something much less calculated than that. Just like me with my Goose, when he saw her with her father at a bar in the Royal Exchange he knew instantly that she was the wife he would love for the rest of his life. The strangest thing was, considering his own striking looks, what attracted her most about him was that he didn't laugh and didn't make jokes. She hated the silly boyishness of most young men she met, the tendency in those days to hide one's personality under a veneer of public school jokiness that made light of both problems and success, a democracy of chums and good fellows. In that culture Dad's school had failed to understand his peculiar learning difficulties. So it was fortunate that in running away from the Queen and her war in Aden, by pure serendipity he landed in Switzerland where his head for figures combined with manual dexterity was recognised by horrible Mrs Hein and developed by Hein himself.

And of course, that he didn't tell jokes didn't mean he wasn't extremely witty. Even as a tiny child I knew when he was being fanciful. And he often made fun of Mum. When she didn't get it he'd kiss her hand and thank her for making his life complete.

"That suit you're wearing," said Mum, "I recognise it."

"I hope you don't mind," I said. "I took a few back to Dad's tailor to have them fitted for me."

I didn't say I'd chosen this light mohair because I remembered him wearing it the last time all of us were visiting the Sibyl together. I wondered if the Sibyl would remember it too.

Of course she did. She eyed me critically.

"When your father wore that suit he was at the height of his power. You may be physically as well-built at nineteen as he was at thirty-nine but it was his personality that filled it out — simply dazzling!"

"There were only two occasions during our marriage that I felt jealous about my husband," said Mum, "the first was on our wedding day when all the girls — especially the Swiss contingent who had flown over uninvited, or at least they were not on Mother's guest list whatever arrangement they may have had with the bridegroom — flirted outrageously with him and he was enjoying it quite shamelessly..."

Including the attack by *Lekkerbek* chilli sauce, I surmised.

"And the other was here at Gus and your house-warming party, Sibylla. That was his thirty-ninth birthday and he was quite euphoric with that inner glow — which should have warned us — it was the last time before he went away for good ..."

"You too were looking absolutely beautiful in your blue-grey summer outfit, Angel," said the Sibyl, "and you came in with your arms full of the little toddly twins so sweet in their floppy sun-hats. All the women there envied you, even I who had my little girls and Willie... it was before Felix Leo was born."

"I decided not to stay for his midnight feast," said Mum. "I was alarmed by his extravagant mood and took the children home..."

But not me. I asked his permission to stay and hid under the library steps in the Archive while the grown-ups talked. When Dad caught me he took me out on the loggia to point out volcanic dust from Mount St Helen's as a red halo around the setting sun. I was frightened and sneaked after him and the Sibyl down to Dr Johnson's teahouse...

Love Incarnate!

I felt it again, the Divine Sibyl's smile embracing me.

"I like wearing this suit," I said, defending myself from the unspoken accusation of hubris, "it's as if Dad is still with me, shedding a bit of stardust on my personality too."

I was actually surprised at how well the women remembered and how much importance they attached to it.

"Dear Connie," said the Sibyl, "You too can be a star, but not the way your Dad was. Like your mother you are simply too nice a person. Wear all his lovely suits, you'll look great and you'll grow into them in your own way."

I blamed it on being the eldest and not having red hair. All the blond loveliness and angelic virtue of Mum couldn't make up for making me too nice a person. But I'd prove the Sibyl wrong. It wouldn't be only his suits that made me whom I wanted to be.

Then my heart did its skippity-jump act as Augusta the Goose came in.

"I thought you were still at school," I said after a blamelessly restrained kiss. The loveliest girl in the world, she had that perfect combination, a curly cloud of Mediterranean hair with the Sibyl's blue eyes and fair skin, melancholy and sunshine in equal measures — invitingly cuddly round breasts and tiny waist, but I could never hurl my body on her in a fuck-frenzy as if she were a Mirta or a Maddie... the Sibyl said that Goosie came as a result of the worst mistake she made during her chequered love-life. But the adorable child she got out of it made the misery of it all worthwhile.

"Officially, school is where I am," she said, "but when May told me you'd be here I had to come and see you."

Earlier Roger phoned me to say that after the elections in South Africa he had persuaded Maddie to take her best *Lekkerbekken* home with him to Zürich. He was renting part of an old brewery and living with her in the management suite above the chilli sauce production plant, leaving the zebu and zebra stew kitchen behind on the veldt to be run by a cooperative of her best students. I refrained from warning my older *broerke* the danger of having his head munched off while feeding his partner's appetite with his no doubt nicely serviceable prick. I had shown the way but had at least had the sense to fuck fast and get out with my head still attached to my genitals. I merely wished him good luck and mentioned I was going to consult the Sibyl about my own prospects.

So within the lapse of a few hours since I casually mentioned my visit to Roger, he had told May and she passed it on to her sister, the message taking on more urgent significance as it hopped its way across all three of us via the phone lines, so now I had my arm around my future wife with our mothers looking on. The workings of Dad's Chaos Theory or the Sibyl Effect?

"When I am going to music academy I could live with Connie in Bayswater," Goosie proposed.

Our mothers said a simultaneous no.

"Finish your education first," they said.

"Childhood sweethearts seldom survive into adulthood," was their verdict.

"We're not children," we protested.

"You've played together all your lives."

Well, that wasn't quite true. I played with May while Goosie skipped around in her own imaginary world that had nothing to do with us. When she played games with anyone it was Willie.

"May was his first sweetheart," said Goosie, "but I've caught up so now it's me."

"No she wasn't," I said. "I was never in love with May."

"But May says you are nice to have real live sex with..."

I was in a quandary. I was so proud of the sensational feeling of power and fulfilment sex with May had given me that I was more inclined to boast about it than deny it, at the same time I was reluctant to admit it to the mothers, especially with Goosie hugging me to demonstrate her expectation that, now she had me, I'd be equally nice to her.

I glanced in the mirror to see which face I had on. Was it that cheerful boy face I had presented to the world until recently or was it the long-jawed serious face than went with Dad's suit, that had been strong enough to risk life and limb fucking the Afrikaans lioness? I could only be relieved that Mrs Hein hadn't taken a fancy to me. That would be the ultimate test of nerve... my mind lingered for a moment on the possibility of facing up to that challenge...

"Con darling," said Mum, "these girls are like sisters to you. It's not proper to play silly games with them."

But that's where the mothers' judgements differed.

"They are not the same," said the Sibyl. "you can say that about May, but not Goosie. She was never anything like a sister. Willy and Felix are her brothers, not Con."

"None of that matters," I said, putting on my long jaw-face. The suit was working. "I'll soon be twenty-one. I'll have my office up and running and we'll be getting married. I can wait."

"But I can't," Goosie wailed.

"Yes you can, we'll do it together."

We went out to walk around the park leaving the mothers to discuss the perils of child lovers. Goosie wanted to question me about May, but I said:

"You know exactly what May and I are like, whether we're having fun or fighting. Well, sex is the same only a bit more."

"I just want to know if you'd tell me the same as May tells me about you."

I could do nothing but hold and hug her.

"Is it the same?" I asked.

Goosie smiled. "You'll have to show me a bit more than that."

I thought of the little gazebo, half-way up the hill between a clump of trees and the view over the fields, Dr Johnson's tea-house. That was where I had peered through the slats to watch my Dad and Goosie's Mama, the irresistible Divine Sibyl, making love. I had knelt in the grass imagining I was the knight at the gate protecting Dad while his guard was down, doing his thing with the magic banshee. My role model.

Dr Johnson may have spent hours in tranquil contemplation of the rustic scene in front of him, but we weren't looking out, we gazed in, seeing only each other.

Anticipating The Goose's arrival, Joe had moved out of his bedroom upstairs, preferring to sleep down beside the garden room where he had his studio. Down there he could paint to loud music without it penetrating to the rest of the house. I too made a definite decision to sleep on Dad's Napoleonic camp bed. Beside the study I had the dressing-room with Dad's shirts, suits, and hand-made shoes, and his bathroom with its array of bottles and tubes of stuff so I could smell a bit like him even though I had a naturally bland body smell, less distinctive than the spicy red-head one I seemed to remember. But best of all, there I found his flint-sharp cutthroat razor that once belonged to the original Conrad, my great-grandfather.

I loved it that I could give new life and meaning to these possessions that were once an essential part of him. They wanted to live on in style and I'd do well enough to serve their purpose.

I quickly reorganised the two now empty front rooms and bathroom as bedroom and sitting-room for the Goose so Uncle Paul and Aunt Madge couldn't take advantage and expand into them. They already had the whole attic floor as well as their sitting-room overlooking the garden. The bulldog's lift came up on the outside wall beside the chimney, unloading him at the landing window.

"It's also handy for not carrying our shopping up five floors," said Madge.

It would do nicely for the Goose when she came.

But the mothers didn't give in.

Mum told me that during the two years she and my Dad were engaged, he too was working at building up his business while she was studying at her academy in Geneva. He came to visit her as often as possible but, until they were married and could live together in their own home, their intimacy confined itself to dancing and a modest goodnight kiss. Only after Dad survived the *Lekkerbek* attack and Mum got over her jealous outrage, did sex play its essential part in getting us boys to create the perfect happy family.

When I tested the implied virtue of this scenario against the Sibyl's opinion she merely smiled and said, "Your Mum has a very rosy picture of the world. I doubt she ever understood that your fine house is the fruit of some discreetly daring smuggling, and it was probably not a great strain on your Dad's libido either, since his side-line in diamonds was done with the cooperation of Maddie at one end and Mrs Hein at the other, who were both only too happy to combine business with pleasure — in fact they were extremely jealous of your mother, his impeccable English fiancée."

"And you?"

"For heavens sake, while your father was enjoying *aardvark braai* with Black Widow for desert, I was squatting under a bush in Ranelagh Road getting an itchy rash from eating too many furry green gooseberries."

The Sibyl was afraid it was not a prophesy but her own wishful thinking that saw us, Conrad and Augusta, in a long and happy marriage, so she sent Goosie to audition for the *Konservatorium* in Bern, just up the street from *Totenkopf* so she and May could live together. Not only did the Goose get a place, but one of her teachers offered the sisters the use of an apartment she owned but temporarily didn't need. It was in an iconic 1960's settlement in the woods, the high-earning Swiss equivalent of a hippy community, almost.

"Damn it," I said when I went to see it. "The Sibyl's daughters again! Whatever Dad said about Luck and Chaos Theory, you have the Divine Sibyl behind you pulling the celestial strings."

"Well, so have you," said May. "Didn't she suckle you in infancy?"

"Only with a bottle of Nestlé baby formula," I protested, blushing at the thought of the Divine Tits. May was quoting Uncle Paul in one of his more indiscreetly frivolous moods and I gave her the Sibyl's stock answer.

Though the complex of interlocked individual homes with open terraces and little gardens was designed for maximum privacy, I was disturbed when May said, "Doors are closed only when people are having sex."

"You too?"

Goosie giggled, "We would if you'd stay to do it for us."

"Grimsi wants to come too as our bodyguard," said May. "The cheek of him. I tell him we are quite well able to make up our own minds in such matters."

I walked away, down towards the bus-stop still not sure what I should understand to be the truth. Cryptic was another thing they'd learned from their mother. Half-way down I stopped and turned back.

"Augusta, you are a diabolical tease," I shouted to her from the doorway. "Will you marry me — now?"

"Certainly not with a casual bonk on the door-mat," Goosie shouted back. "I can't possibly do it without proper ceremony."

I was jubilant, taking that for a positive yes.

"We'll get May and Broer Roger to be witnesses," I said.

"... and your Yummy Aphrodite of the Pickled Zebu Cock can come,"

said the Goose, "and bring us a feast — as long as it does not include anything reptile, insect or foul guts. A nicely cooked goose would do."

So that was how we were married. Roger and Maddie arrived with all
speed in Maddie's Landrover bringing a variety of *Lekkerbekken* in the back,
Roger wrote out a certificate in the traditional Swiss ethos in four languages,
signed it with May and Maddie, and a couple of the neighbours just to be
sure, witnesses that we swore to be lovers to the end of time. Maddie produced an enormous spicy pie filled with quite ordinary free-range chicken
and certified welfare veal, mushrooms and spinach, served with mustard
and pickled gherkins, enough to feed any passing neighbours who were
encouraged by May to join in, determined to make it an big occasion for us.

That's how my life as married man began. It just happened. Not as
I imagined, a planned affair between Goosie and me, but better, with Roger
and May taking the occasion out of my hands, telling me all that was
required of me was to take my bride to bed and make her happy.

"As soon as it's done I'll phone Mama," said May. "I'll tell her there was no
point in postponing what's inevitable."

The pledge I gave my wife was to fill her to the brim with my love and
that is how it was: the more I gave the more I wanted to give and my sweetheart confirmed our bond with little affirmative murmurs, accepting me
as her lover for life, pulsating with pleasure until I could give no more.

We could hear voices and laughter from the friends and neighbours
outside so we went out and joined in the feast.

"I told you he'd be nice," said May to dreamy-eyed Goosie when she
brought her a plate of meringue with squished raspberries and chocolate
sauce, a gift from their neighbour. "He's good, he knows how to start and
when to stop. Of course, he's had some exceptional practice ..."

Goosie followed May's glance in the direction of Maddie who was tossing
off the *mousseux du Valais* kindly supplied by another resident from his
generous cellar, and together the sisters giggled, as the picture they formed
of a long-limbed, courteously polite youth like me grappling with She,
the white African Queen, struck them as fantastically incongruous.

"Roger has her now," said May. "That's even more fantastic. They make a great working partnership with the sex fired up by fiery chilli. I wonder how long before they are entirely burnt up. One of these days there'll be nothing left but a bubbling cauldron and a pile of hot ash ..."

As the sisters became more and more consumed with laughter it occurred to me that, now that Roger was being slowly consumed by the praying mantis, May no longer had a partner, not that it seemed to trouble her in the least, she certainly showed no jealousy about either Roger or me. We were what we had always been, her prime comrades. What we did with our man-bits was no more than incidental.

Maybe that's where Grimsi came in, unlikely as it seemed. Not a thought I dared entertain for fear of letting my imagination run riot.

The neighbours stayed to fête us until 10:30 when they all went off to bed to be up in good time to swim or do their yoga before the 30-minute cycle that separated their idyll from the rest of the world. May and Goosie too, they had unquestioningly taken on the same strict routines of work and study.

Having done our marriage act quite exhaustively earlier it was nice to get into bed with my wife in a relaxed state of mind — only it didn't stay relaxed. As soon as her adorable plumply slim little body inserted itself into my embrace I completely lost my head and heart all over again and went at that tender young pussy as if she were a well-oiled whore like Mirta or the man-eating lioness Maddie. Goosie's startled cries spurred me on until I came to an abrupt finish with a bellow of satisfaction at my own indomitable spirit.

"Wow!" said Goosie, "That was quite a deep fuck. You must have been saving that one up for a special occasion:"

Coming to my senses, ashamed of my loss of control, I said: "I don't know what came over me. I didn't mean to give you such a battering, I'm truly sorry, my gentle sweet love!"

Goosie said nothing but snuggled up into my arms and slept, or seemed to though she sighed in her sleep as I, unable to rest, continued to stroke and caress the lovely young person confided to my care. Keeping my touch as light as a feather I explored her curves and hollows, choking on my insatiable desire for her.

Mirta said I fucked like my father. Maybe it was his wandering spirit fused with mine — if so, I'd have to harness his fuck-lust to appropriate situations — Goosie's so-called special occasions. Eventually I joined her in sleep with my hand cupped protectively over the precious puss.

When I woke up Goosie was up and dressed and ready to go to her Konservatorium.

"Come back to London with me," I said.

"Not in the middle of the term," she said. "My professors would think I wasn't taking my study seriously."

So, after a day and a night of marriage we broke up again.

I didn't want to go straight home to London. I knew the mothers would gang up against me, I need expect no sympathy from them, so I decided to stop over in Basel City and see if I couldn't unearth the faithful Gladys and drag her out of her house-proud retirement. I needed her now. If anyone could relieve us of the painfully slow unlocking of Dad's mysterious connections — I was doing not so badly but I was frustrated by the suspicion of what I might be missing. My reading at LSE made me aware of the vast potential of the world out there and I was in a hurry to claim my share of it.

I thought of visiting Mr Hein in his office, where he might be more inclined to take me seriously — after all, he had employed my father at 19, recognising his genius when no one else was taking him seriously, saw he was at least worth more than cannon fodder for Arabs.

However, when I found my way past reception up to the head office, it was Mrs Hein there in command,

"Hein is in the Galapagos," she said. "How can I help you?"

"I'm looking for Gladys," I said.

I didn't expect an answer. Hein might have informed me, but Mrs Hein...?

"You may take me out to lunch," she said.

I was going to be made pay for any help I received.

As I feared, Mrs Hein's attitude over some trout-like river fish was mockingly flirtatious. Was she luring me on to make a fool of myself? Was getting in touch with Gladys going to be worth the humiliation?

An excellent piece of Appenzeller and a carafe of Humagne eased my caution and I gave in to the feeling I was letting Dad have his way, making use of my cock for his own satisfaction. I was sure that was what happened when so against my Mumsy nature I gave Goosie that amazing 'deep fuck' she recognised as something different. I had seen him do it with Goosie's Mama, howling with passion, giving up the ghost in an agony of desire.

"Were you and my father lovers?" I asked bluntly, to make Mrs Hein acknowledge what she was doing to me.

Her laughter was a bell, clear and melodious.

"More than that," she said. "I'm your step-mother."

This had me completely foxed.

"How?"

"Your father and I were married for five years. Obviously long before you were born. He was 19, just like you, and the most gorgeous, innocently sexy boy one could imagine. All the girls were crazy for him but he was too shy to take advantage of it — losing his mother so young and half his life-time in boys' schools didn't help — until I rescued him from their harassment. He was simply the best; sweet face, beautiful boyish body and a cock to die for..."

To die for: that was what Mirta said too, but twenty years later it was in more literally true circumstances...

"Just like you," Mrs Hein said, eyeing me suggestively.

"All I want is to find Gladys," I said. "I don't know her surname, didn't she marry someone Swiss?"

Mrs Hein's bell-like laugher rang out again.

"Practical as always," she said. "Your clever Dadi married me because he couldn't go back to England so he needed a Swiss passport. 5 years later when he got what he wanted we divorced — by mutual consent as is done in Switzerland. No tiresome litigation."

"And Roger?"

"He came later, I teased a baby out of him. Such a stud, he couldn't resist the offer. Your Uncle Toby is supposed to keep track of you all for the inheritance... but he specifically excluded Roger, who gets nothing because, he said, Hein stole some of his best ideas."

"He got the Totenkopf ring," I said, knowing it would annoy her.

"I bought it for him, more appropriate than a proper wedding ring.

So Roger really was my brother, something I surmised all along. Celtic Fringe x European Jew gave him more emphatic looks and personality than my whiter than white Anglo-Celt. Roger was successful in everything he undertook; I had suffered two catastrophic failures so far. Instead of burying a body I had raised a ghost, and I had married a wife I couldn't hold. On the other hand my business was growing. I'd do everything necessary to succeed.

Incest even, if that's what it took.

"Dad's other women say I fuck just like him," I said.

Chagrin! Other women indeed!

I could see it in the set of her mouth though she didn't blink.

"I have to get back to the office now," she said, "but if you want to know more about Gladys I'll look her up for you in our records. Come to my place for dinner."

"With pleasure," I said and saw her to the door before returning to my table to finish my coffee. While I was idly looking at the display of fish in the vitrine nicely labelled with their pedigrees, I had a sudden picture in my mind of the trio, Dad at the top then Eggers and Gladys, united against the background of Dad's mysterious, magic hive of industry.

Then when Dad sold his workplace and design studio Eggers had taken over a number of Dad's patents to put them into production on his own account. So I asked for a phone book and worked my way through it until I found the most likely firm: Eggerswill Machina AG.

I took a walk along the river, found the address and went in. I asked in my best Baseler Düütch, "Where's Gladys?"

I was handed a phone.

A rather snappy voice asked "What now? Or maybe it was "Wasss t nüü?" Not a lot of difference when said in Welsh.

The Voice from the Valleys on the Phone. No wonder Mum got annoyed with it, especially when it came between her and her husband.

"I'm Conrad and I've come over from the Bayswater office to have a look at Dad's accounts."

"Which?"

I recognised a test question of a Grimsi nature.

"All, but particularly pharmaceuticals."

"You want to know why the Mexican yams are not yielding so well any more. Well, I'll tell you — that Concho is useless but no one seems to have the welly to give him the boot. It's about time you got in there and told him to stop parading the *Black Madonna* around the fields and use some natural predators instead. Mosquito-eating frogs in other words, or smoke bombs. And to stop selling 'surplus' on the side for food. There is no surplus. We use all we can get..."

I learned more in 30 minutes from the Voice than in months of fiddling around with tapes and Pepe. But I still couldn't quite fit in Scletti with his frogs. Why did we need two lots of frogs? Maybe slim yellow and big fat green — or *visa versa*. I'd have to go and see for myself. Too bad about the Goose. It would have been fun to go frog-hunting together.

I was still running the conversation with Gladys through my mind when it was time to go and settle with Mrs Hein. Claiming to be my step-mother! What would Mum say about that? Not that I'd tell her, it was too rude.

The Heins at home lived in the two top floors of a 5-floor apartment house.

Will you walk into my parlour? said the spider to the fly...

one of the Sibyl's many nursery rhymes she sang to me when I was little.

Mrs Hein had set an intimate small corner of a very long dining table with a nice array of glasses and cutlery. Why did I find this surprisingly sexy? It was on the tip of my tongue to say she needn't have bothered, that I had already found Gladys so she didn't have to play the step-mother act with me any more. It was sheer mischievousness that I held my tongue and played along with this fantasy. The very deception was arousing and I was brimming with glee to see how it would play itself out.

A small dish of smoked eel was placed between us and two glasses of flowery Johannisberg Mont d'Or. We shared the slivers of eel and I felt the wine stirring in my head and giving my balls a delightfully rosy glow.

Her plot, I figured, was get me flushed up as quickly as possible, all the better to make me lose my head and show me up for a foolishly susceptible youth. Maybe that was how she had captured my Dad when he was young and inexperienced in the wiles of women. I'd make it up to him.

When she went into the kitchen to bring out two tiny medallions of steak and a bottle of Blau Burgunder I followed her and tore one of the medallions in half to eat in one bite, giving her the other half. She hesitated about following my example, but as I held two delicately small glasses of the deep purple wine ready, she went along with having the sequence of our dinner dictated by me. The second steak torn in half, two bites each, two more mini-imbibes and we were ready to move on to the real purpose of the evening.

Sex.

But not sex as she proposed it, luring on the silly young man to expose himself to her teasing and taunting, instead, following rules laid down by me, fly unzipped, knickers down, and a flying fuck free-standing with only each other for support. She had to cling to me, I had to hold on to her, her leg hitched up out of the way. I had never done it like this before but it came with complete ease, without hitch or hesitation.

Her reaction surprised me. Clasping her hands between her thighs to ease out the stretch or the itch, she was looking at me with dismay.

"How did you know?" she asked.

"What?"

"That's what he did, exactly so. At your mother's wedding no less, as if paying off old scores with his first wife before settling in with his new one. He never forgave me for divorcing him so I could marry Hein, said I was in love with money — that was when he was employed at SIG, a good salary but no fortune — but my so-called betrayal was what spurred him on to leave a safe job behind him and set out on his own adventures. I should have known he'd make good..."

"Obviously you did him a favour by getting out of his life," I said, zipping up, somewhat bemused by her version of events. I thought I knew exactly what I was doing and why, but her words suggested it was Dad again, his pre-emptive strike acting to protect me from the betrayal he had suffered at her hands.

I could feel his pain at losing her, a high-flying, attractive, clever woman, I could feel how I myself would crave that bitter-sweet excitement. I chuckled inside. Though never named in so many words, I'd probably heard stories from Dad's youthful first marriage without taking in its significance — indeed, now that I understood it, I remembered that Meg and the Sibyl used to discuss with whispers and suppressed giggles the incident of the knickers dropped behind the study door and who might or might not have seen them, including Grandfather and Mr Hein himself. As a child, knickers on the floor weren't so important, May chucked hers around with abandon.

Stooping to pick them up would be undignified, an acknowledgement of defeat even, so the scrap of black textile remained where it was as a silent witness while Mrs Hein and I resumed our interrupted dinner seated on a small lady-with-pug-sized sofa, she spooning out mouthfuls of chocolate cheesecake while my hands were busy re-acquainting him with the trim body he once knew only too well, apple tits and tight cunny.

She's leading me into another trap, I surmised.

"My Dad delighted in the challenge of a slitty entry squeezing his heroic dick."

"How can you possibly know that?"

I didn't know how I knew, I just did.

"I feel it in my fingers," I said, standing up.

I produced two small cups of expresso from the machine.

"I know where your Gladys lives," she said. "I can take you there in the morning."

"Is that an invitation to stay the night?" I asked.

"Yes," she said.

I was jubilant. A whole night of Heini cock-fighting — did the Hein woman know that her Roger was *de facto* husband to one of his father's other ex-lovers and having to produce the same level of performance to satisfy her?

While his Mami was in the bathroom I phoned Roger.

"Your mother has just asked me to stay the night."

"What do you mean?"

"I don't think we'll get to bed. I rather fancy her on the terrace by moon-light or sweating it out in the sauna…"

"Don't you dare," he said and slammed the phone down. Zürich to Basel — that gave me about three hours to have fun. I figured mine and Dad's stamina would last that long.

Ours was longer than Mrs Hein's. When Roger arrived she was lying asleep in the arms of the giant wooden figure that overlooked the city from the edge of the Hein terrace.

"Why didn't you bring Maddie?" I asked. "They could have compared the merits of youthful lovers."

I had dressed myself with my usual care and was ready to go. A confront-ation between Roger and his mother would be entertaining, but even more appealing was the thought of her waking up naked and alone in the lap of the gods, wondering how she got there, then the uncertain recollection of the night's events, asking herself if she had dreamt me.

"Come on," I said to Roger. "Let's get out of here."

We drove away together in the *Lekkerbekken* Landrover. It was hard to read Roger's expression.

"That's a rather odd sculpture," I remarked, "displayed rather menacingly on the terrace: a stocky, muscular man-figure with a chunky wooden penis, I've noticed the Swiss aesthetic sense runs to the chunky and functional but pubic hair expressed as nubbly curls whittled out of nutty wood is quite extreme. Your mother was cuddling up to it when she drifted off in blissful anticipation of the next bout with my more flexible human-sized one. I hope she doesn't feel lonely when she wakes up."

"It's Hercules. Dadi Hein bought it — he sees it as a portrait of himself," was Roger's stiffly formal explanation. "Dadi's name is Hercule though he never lets anyone call him that — my mother is not a promiscuous woman, anything but! But you remind her of Him..."

"Smiley? Well I know now why as a young man he had to escape her."

"He didn't escape her, Opi Bott had to bribe the uncircumcised pig to go away and get lost. He didn't want me as a grandson."

"With a top-notch Porsche? So Smiley took the bribe and his freedom, and Opi still got landed with a red-headed pig of a grandson. Smiley the trickster!"

"Let's stop for breakfast," said Roger, turning into the rail station.

"She's a tricksy woman, your Mami," I said when we sat down with our selection of breads, cheeses and jams. We had the same taste in breakfast, ever since we were little at the Palace with Smiley.

"I spend my life dodging her," said Roger. "But it's embarrassing that you had her like that. I never saw her naked before, it was quite a shock. I hope she gets down off Hercule safely. Oh, my God, suppose she slips and goes tumbling down into the bushes below!"

"It's too late to go back now," I said, and to distract him from the dire possibility that Mrs Hein would have to walk back up through the garden like a prelapsarian Eve, added:

"She's terrifically sexy and after all, she's the same age as the *Lekkerbek* Maddie."

"I keep explaining that Maddie and I are business partners..."

"With the sex as by-product, I know..."

"But I'll probably marry her to keep her and her business legal.

Officially registered, as one does in Switzerland, not a fantasy like you and the Goose."

"You made a great registrar nevertheless," I said. "I'll take the train from here, *Broerke*, and tell your Mami next time you see her that I had already found out all I need to know from Gladys the Voice, so bribing me for sex was quite unnecessary. But thank her anyway, an experience I wouldn't have missed for all the frogs in China."

When I arrived home in London Mum was having an argument with the twins. They were standing side by side wearing brown robes and wooden crucifixes on their chests and saying they didn't like School. They wanted to go to their monastery of the Holy Innocents instead.

"At School we have to follow silly rules and customs, at the Innocents we make the rules."

"That's nonsense," said Mum. "It's the Reverent Father Abbot who makes the rules."

"But he listens to us. All he wants is to go to Heaven to be with Jesus and we tell him what Jesus is like. And they let us get out of bed in the middle of the night to do a bit of singing. At School they're always telling us to keep quiet."

Mum looked at me in despair as if it were all my fault. Ever since they came back from Buenos Aires they'd been obstreperous.

"Tell your brothers they need to get properly educated first."

"You're clever," I said to them. "You can skip through School at top speed and be out of there in no time. You need to know everything to be able to work really good miracles."

"We can look it up in books."

"That's far too slow," I said. "You need to be able to give answers quick as a flash of inspiration, so you need to have it all ready in your head."

The twins were reluctant to admit I was right though they liked the flash of inspiration bit.

"Let's go and consult the Sibyl," said Mum, wisely moving it on to the highest authority.

The Sibyl was as usual in her place surrounded by the lugubrious Virtues — only Caritas looked cheerful, enjoying other people's misfortunes. May was there too, so while Mum explained the problem of the best school in the world against a troop of fanatic old men, May and I went for a walk.

"Grimsi is jealous." May explained her own problem.

"Good grief, what of?" I asked, smiling at the picture this gave me of the cantankerous little man.

"He liked me living in the Kügelhöfli — and there is actually plenty of room, it's surprisingly spacious under the medieval rafters. He's like a watchdog, he could keep an eye on me there but now I'm outside the city in the wilderness with the Silly Goose anything can happen — probably, more than anything, meet a man I like better than him."

"Good grief!"

Again.

"I'm somewhat sex starved," said May, eyeing me speculatively. "Roger told me you well and truly screwed his mother — in more than one sense."

"And," I said, "so?"

"He was a bit Swiss-embarrassed but then when we tried to imagine how you, with all your amiable Geneva politesseiness, could get your dick up that ice-cold diamond-studded slit we nearly died laughing."

I was greatly relieved that it struck my confrères as funny rather than rude or perverse. May understood how offended I was when Mami Hein taunted me with being my step-mother. A spot of shameful incest seemed the best response at the time.

"And actually it was wildly arousing, I had a fantastic fuck. Did you tell Augusta?"

"I don't discuss you with her. That's your affair, but if you want to know, she is quite happy to refer to you as her husband."

I was so happy I kissed May as proxy.

"Do you think we three are doomed not to have normal happy love lives?" asked May, kissing back by way of feeding her starved libido.

"Roger seems to be well satisfied with his arrangement."

"Like my Daddy was happy enough until he met Mama and discovered true love... "

Geneva politesseiness aside, I was on the point of thumping May for daring to suggest my Mum wasn't his truest love but I remembered in time our unspoken agreement. My Dad and her Daddy were two different people.

"Your Dad always reminded you you're not allowed to hit, thump or kick girls," said May, grinning at me.

"And you certainly took advantage of it. Can I kiss you again instead?"

"I wonder if after all you aren't really my true love," said May, sighing. "Let's go up to Dr Johnson's tea-house."

When we were strolling back to hear the Sibyl's verdict on the Innocents, I said:

"I do love you, May, and you're a deeply satisfying lay, but honestly I adore the Goose about a million times more."

"I'm too fucked out to kick you but you deserve it, you ballsy bastard."

"I'm the only one who isn't," I pointed out.

The Divine Sibyl pointed out to Axie and Boris that Rosita and Camilla wouldn't be allowed to visit them if they shut themselves up at the Holy Innocents, and that I was right about needing to know all there was to know in one's head.

"Your father did, he was truly a polymath and he didn't need books. He had that Tower of Babel trick of building a tower of knowledge in his mind, whizzing up a spiral slope at lightening speed to find the right level where he had a particular piece of information stacked away, and adding an extra level when he ran out of space. He must have reached the stratosphere and that's why we can't see him any more."

"That's it," said Axie.

"Yes, up there people become transparent, you only know they're there when you bump into them." Boris was building his own vision.

"We can get that high too," said Axie.

"Better than going to Heaven...

... and they went away babbling about their personal Babylon, and how they would put in lifts to get Rosita and Camilla up from level to level and maybe halfway up keep a goat and some chickens, moving them higher up as the tower grew taller.

That seemed to have solved the School question — for the moment anyway.

I intended to stay behind with May, content that we could find mutual solace in our sex-starved lives, but the Sibyl made that impossible too.

"You two will have to stop inflicting me with your love lives," she said.

"We never mention our love lives," we protested in unison.

"I can't help seeing what you mean to each other," said the Sibyl. "Especially you, Conrad. You exude sex."

Mum looked quite shocked.

"Surely not, Sibylla. Con is the soul of discretion, he couldn't be more modest and decorous."

"He's a handsome, healthy young man, the natural epitome of sexual desire, love is in every fibre of his being."

"I love him," said May.

"But I'm married to Augusta," I said, not to let any doubt creep in.

"So I'll have to make do with Grimsi — for now anyway."

"You see what I'm complaining about," said the Sibyl. "I can't resolve your conflicts for you. If you want to shack up with a gnome, May, you may well be perfectly happy, but if Conrad wants to be married to Goosie he has to wait until she's ready."

"Your father waited two years for me," Mum reminded me.

I couldn't tell them about Dad's ex-lovers who were wantonly using me as substitute for his heroic fuck tool — not that I wasn't more than willing to comply, so the Sibyl must be right about me. I couldn't help smiling at the vision of Mami Hein's naked body lolling fearlessly against her wooden Hercule on the edge off the abyss and Maddie tawny-skinned in the flickering flame-stripes on the African hearthrug... such terrific females!

"Just look at him!" said the Sibyl, laughing at me and annoyed at the same time, "that smile!"

"You should be blind-folded, Sibyl," I said. "It's not fair that you read me as if my thoughts were written on my face."

"They are, sweetheart," she said, "I've known you from the day you were born, I could tell from your little face when you were wetting your pants or if you'd been stealing jam. And what you do now is just the same only more age-appropriate."

It wasn't Mum or the Sibyl I was heeding when I spent the next two years pursuing my career, but following the Voice's advice. She also sent me the little list of Dad's agents from the time before the phone went silent. So in between exams at the LSE I was away supervising the work in the field with Pepe and Schletti, Pepe developing our fungus farm in Mexico in addition to getting our yam plantation back into full production, and in Basel Schletti who was in charge of our small, secret and esoteric laboratory, researching and processing the precious serums and crystals. Since my Dad's time yams had come into widespread use for producing bio-identical hormones, but we still won on quality, and now the race was on to find the most lucrative use for our frog fungus.

Mum accepted my travels without question. She was used to Dad's coming and going and needed no explanations. She surprised me by handing me a set of tapes, saying someone had given them to her some time ago, thinking she'd be interested in saving Dad's talks on ethics before magnetic tape went out use.

"The archivist said I should consider publishing, but oh, dear," she sighed, "some of the most boring evenings of my life were spent when I had to sit beside him looking beautiful — I never understood why people considered him an entertaining speaker at events. He had endless stories he'd heard from his grandfather Conrad, a lifetime of triumphs and disasters, all sorts of shady dealings during the Great Depression, before and during the war, some quite dreadful but it seemed amusing to them... wickedly slanderous but he always managed to stay out of range from lawsuits though he was often threatened. He was positively disappointed that no one dared pursue him — in private he was so reserved, he'd have relished the excuse to show his wit in the formality of a court."

I listened to the tapes, entranced to hear his distinctive voice, and undertook the task of writing them up. As I wrote I found myself arguing with him and and updating the talks for my own use. I was sitting at my desk tapping out my latest two-fingered essay on the devious ways ideas can be stolen and words twisted and falsified, feeling satisfied that I could both reason and write adequately in spite of the inadequacies of my parents, when I heard a sound outside in the street that puzzled me, remotely familiar but unlikely. I went out on the balcony to look down, and saw, to my amazement, Dad's Jaguar parked at the door.

I was still staring in utter stupefaction when out stepped Willy and waved up at me with huge grin on his face.

"I don't know what's in the boot," he said when I rushed down. "I didn't open it. Here's the key."

"How on earth did you get it here?" I asked. Willy was only fifteen and didn't look in the least mature for his age.

"I found the key in Uncle Toby's safe — I've been able to pick that safe since I was ten — so I smuggled in cans of petrol from the farm shop until I'd filled the tank, washed the dust and barn-owl dirt off with the yard hose, put on a James Hunt cap and Porsche sunglasses and just drove straight here. It was easy. I borrowed the tax disk from the Rolls we inherited from the Ancient of Days when he died in his Tower, Father only ever uses it when he has to go to funerals so unless some old dude dies he won't miss it."

I took the key with trepidation, almost in tears.

"I never dared think I really wanted the Jaguar, but now it's here I'm just overwhelmed."

I ran my hand over the bonnet.

"Yes, she's a beauty," said Willy. "Built before BL took over and made a balls-up of the production line. I'll help you get her back into condition if you want me to. I identified what needs doing on the drive here. Nothing serious."

While he was chatting on about the mechanics I was nervously approaching the boot. That was where my real interest lay. It might be empty or it might be a treasure trove.

Boxes.

Leather gun cases. (Bargaining tools for May?)

A lumpy canvas bag.

A pair of well-worn riding boots going stiff from lack of waxing.

A bag of antique gold coins, Conrad's pesos de oro with which Dad had learned to count and calculate.

I concluded that, apart from the boots which had probably been in transit to his cobbler, it really was treasure trove, items he left safe in his underground parking slot at the London penthouse when he was about to go to South America.

Willy helped me carry it all up to my room, and there it was, two gun cases with a pair of hunting rifles in each, signed with the *Totenkopf* emblem, 1979, probably the last ones he made, and loose in a canvas bag the precious Sturmgewehr, model early 1960's, that May so badly wanted. But now I had it in my hands I knew I couldn't part with it. I didn't need anything else. Let her keep all the rest. I was almost sorry I didn't qualify to follow his career in the *Armee*, it seemed so right that a man should be equipped to defend his land and people while at the same time doing his every-day work and earning a living.

Willy counter-argued, "We pay our surplus of naturally so inclined yobs and bully-boys to do that for us. It keeps them from being a nuisance to the rest of us."

"But," I said, "my Dad ran away from being conscripted into the wrong kind of war, yet he absolutely saw the point of the Swiss Army and loved it. I think I would too but it's too late now. If only he had got me a Swiss passport when I was little like May. What are your plans for the Grim Tower?"

"You are not going to blow it up," said Willy. "My great-grandfather lived there happily until he fell down drunk on his 101st birthday... so will I. The gallery at the top with the painted roof-beams is a terrific room and it's handy enough for Oxford."

"But the Sibyl says the Ancient was quite mad," I said, thinking how appropriate it was he fell to his death down the ancestral stairwell. Not that I cared any more about the blowing-up. Paul and I had finished our script for the *Downfall of Tyranny* and when we had the spare time and money to produce it we'd fake the end in the usual way. All theatre is illusion, exemplified by the Tempest.

"I'll put in a massive sound system and have the *Eroica* blasting away from top to bottom, that should be enlightened enough for you. Do you want me to leave the Jaguar here or drive it down to our place so I can work on it?"

"I can't legally let you drive it," I said. "I'd be responsible."

"Look the other way and I'll steal it."

"Your Dad is a highly respected barrister who is bound to become a judge soon but it looks as if you are heading for a life of crime."

"Well, your Dad skimmed along the edge of the law quite successfully, so..." looking at the gun collection and the bag of gold, "I don't see why I can't do the same."

When May came to see me I kept the gun cabinet locked so she couldn't go snooping to see what I had.

"Mama says Willy stole Daddy's Jag," she said, noncommittally testing how much I was involved. "Uncle Toby is a bit cross, he says it's really yours but apart from that it was quite mad of Willy to drive it all the way from Dorset to Kent. Willy says he stuck to minor roads. Gus warned him to watch out or he'll get a criminal record and that will be a hindrance in whatever he chooses for his future career. Willy isn't worried, he's too young to go to jail and he can always be a motor mechanic if they won't have him in law school. And there is nothing in the boot but literally a pair of boots."

Well done, Willy! He hadn't admitted his deviation to unload in Bayswater.

I didn't dare ask May what the Goose was doing and she didn't tell me. The Sibyl too seemed deliberately to avoid mentioning her. Such a conspiracy of silence worried me, but I was equally obstinate about not asking. I felt I was somehow trapped into some bargain the terms of which were obscure to me. Maybe I should analyse it following the principles of Dad's business ethics.

May however approached the topic by asking:

"How's your sex life going?"

"It isn't," I said, "as you know perfectly well."

"How would I know?" said May.

I turned away from her.

"I've no one either," she said. "Roger is attached to that old witch he's still quite ludicrously fucking. I think she really must have some love drug she spices his food with."

"He's lucky to have such a splendid woman."

"Why don't you go back to your old whore Mirta then?" said May. "Look at you, barely twenty-two and already such a po-faced Geneva dude... "

"You don't give a damn, really."

"I do, honestly I do love you."

I took May upstairs to show her the set of rooms, stripped of their past history, I had waiting for my wife.

"I've left them bare," I said, "until she comes. Just like my heart. I'm not lonely but without my love it's empty."

But it didn't matter what I was thinking in my head, my stupid cock had a mind of its own, recognising the presence of a familiar lover, and it was after all quite nice to give in to it and a tremendous relief. Also, I realised, I was still jealous that May talked about Roger as if she'd really prefer him.

We three. An isosceles triangle.

Having failed to uncover the truth about Willie and the Jaguar, May departed leaving the door of my room open and now I heard Mum come upstairs. Dad's room, my room, was so well sound-proofed that I wasn't normally aware of life going on in the rest of the house.

"Mum," I called as she was about to go into the drawing-room across the hall. She was carrying a bottle and a dish of chocolate truffles so she must be expecting her friends. Her role in life as a beautiful, rich young widow suited her so perfectly I realised with a stab of fear how devastated I'd be if she ever remarried.

"I'm going to New York next week," I said, "would you like to come with me?"

She looked positively dismayed.

"Oh, Connie dear, all the times your father went there — he loved swanning around trade fairs, not that he ever sold anything, he said that was Eggers job — I never had the least wish to go with him..."

She couldn't bear to say no to me. I didn't give up though and followed her into the drawing-room. It was the feminine counterpart of Dad's study, on the garden side of the house.

"I really should have the garden re-designed," she said looking down at the greenery laid out below. "It became such a barn-yard when you were all children with the goat and the pony ..."

"And your birds."

I was teasing her the way Dad teased her.

"The aviary stays," she said.

"There's a lovely one in Regent's Park," I said. "We can get one like that, give them more room to fly. And we can let live mice run around for them to catch instead of tossing dead ones."

Mollified by my suggestion, Mum said, "You may take me to Paris if you like, my Aunties used to stay at the George V and loved it."

Mum's notorious Aunties, I wondered if she knew the reputation they might have left behind there. I'd be curious to find out.

As soon as we checked in, the elderly porter taking charge of our luggage said to me:

"I see you're not wearing your Hermès hat, Mr Deathridge."

I was about to deny ever wearing a hat outside School when it occurred to me that maybe with cataracts blurring his vision he was seeing me as my Dad. But then, the only hat I'd ever seen Dad wearing was a curly brimmed vintage topper, in a sense of irony, for Ascot and weddings. So mention of an Hermès hat was a mystery.

"I remember you coming across the road wearing it. Your aunts were delighted with how handsome you looked and insisted we all admired it."

"My aunts," said Mum, "they were my aunts, not his. They could be extremely frivolous. My late husband was very patient with them and humoured their whims. This is our eldest son, Conrad."

The apologies were profuse. "I should have known," he said, "but the resemblance is remarkable. *Très drôle!*"

It had to be suit again because without red hair and taller I really wasn't that much like my Dad that I could be mistaken for him, even by blurry eyesight.

"You do become more like him every day," Mum remarked, as if it were so obvious it was hardly worth remarking on.

I had so deliberately cultivated his image, I shouldn't be upset now that I had succeeded. But it did change how I viewed my own life and my future.

"All right," I said, "let's go across the road and see if we can find another like it."

In the shop stacked to the ceiling with beautiful hats, and some elegant young women to help with the selection, I was instantly taken in hand by the hatter himself. Without discussion he took down three to show me. One he discarded at once, leaving me with a choice of two. I let my eyes wander over the great array in the shop and the hatter, seeing my gaze deviate said, square heads, round heads, big noses, small chins, the choice is unlimited, but with your skull, your jaw line so refined, this is the perfect balance."

I saw little difference between the two but the hatter was quite adamant which I had to buy, and then spent a good quarter hour with his block steaming it to the perfect fit. In the meantime Mum was consulting the young women to find a companion piece for her. For formal occasions she tended to get her hats from the Queen's hat man to be on the safe side, with an added feather or veil for a touch of stylish *élan*, so this was quite a departure for her, a shapely felt cloche that gave strength to her flawless face, enhancing her personality. I kissed her the way Dad would have, to express his approval.

While we strolled along the boulevard to find a place for lunch she said: "This alone has made the trip worthwhile. Thank you, Connie dear. And you do look truly distinguished, it's a pity your father would never wear a hat."

Except for the curious incident of the giddy aunts and the Hermès hatter.

Mum's aunts lived in France and we never saw them now, though at one time they had lived in our house while Uncle Toby was finding them a suitable house in France, with Mum waiting patiently for them to depart with their troop of baby boys.

"So tiresome of them both to have twins," Mum complained.

All I remembered about that was that they yearned after a fancy *château* with stone greyhounds running around the high walls which they insisted Dad had promised to buy for them, but as Dad had gone by then and Uncle Toby was in charge, he told them to have some sense and bought an *hôtel* in Normandy instead. I'd thought a proper hotel would be nice for visits but it meant only that it was a rather grand town house. They and Mum had a serious falling out over it and we never went visiting. Uncle Paul went to see them once a year out of duty, it was his kind of work. Odd that the hotel porter at the George V remembered them so clearly.

While at lunch with a three-tiered selection of shell-fish and crustaceans, my eye caught a poster advertising a concert at the Salle Pleyel with some star Japanese pianist, but also, in small letters, the Conservatoire Bernese. Leaving Mum on a terrace to enjoy her desert and coffee I ran to the box office to get tickets for that evening. The only free ones were either right at the back or the corner of the front row, guaranteed to give one a crick in one's neck, but I didn't hesitate.

I took Mum on a river cruise and the entire afternoon prayed to God, the Sibyl, St Nicola, Bishop of Myra, patron of brides, children and thieves, and to anyone else of influence who might be listening.

Mum would have liked a light supper before the concert so she could go to bed early after a long day but I appealed to her sense of what's proper, to make her wait until after for dinner. Then she objected to the seats — your father always got the best seats — but I said, "It's only music. You can keep your eyes closed."

"Your father used to do that, said he just wanted to hear the music and not see the ugly expressions contorting their faces. People always thought he had fallen asleep, it was embarrassing."

"Oh, Mum! Just enjoy it. What does it matter what people think?"

The programme started with preludes from *Parsifal* and *Lohengrin* and though the music reflected perfectly my yearning for my beloved, it went on too long and I stopped hearing anything but the impatient beating of my own heart. Then the Bernese filed on for their piece. I had no idea what they were playing because my eyes were riveted on the first violin. Mum with her eyes closed had really fallen asleep so I could go totally rigid with anxiety, bite my lips, shuffle my feet and generally act like a love-sick goon, and when at long last the lights went up for the interval push my way out to find my sweetheart.

Pure blind instinct found her.

"Goodness," she said, "what are you doing here? I thought you'd be cutting up frogs in the Bay of Mexico."

"I don't cut up frogs, anywhere, ever. When is your concert over?"

"Now. That was my prize piece. Did you like it?"

"I didn't hear a single note. You'll have to play it for me again in private. My Mum is outside in the foyer, come out and give her a polite hello."

Mum was quite happy not to wait for the star turn, that the concert was over as far as we were concerned. I proposed strolling back to the George V but Mum protested she didn't have walking shoes on, so I sent her ahead in a taxi telling her to order the best she could from room service so it would be ready by the time we arrived.

It seemed the most ordinary thing in the world to find myself walking along arm in arm, simply enjoying the bustle of the brightly lit Paris night with my wife — except I didn't know for sure if she were still my wife.

The Goose told me about her tour with her fellow prize pupils ending
with the triumph of performing in Paris. I appreciated the significance that
she had abandoned their celebrations to come with me.

"I told them my husband has come to meet me," she said, as if she had
sent me an invitation and I had dutifully turned up to support her.

When we got up to our suite, Mum had made a splendid effort, following
the advice of the chef since she was not a food-aware person herself.

"I told him to make it nice for my son and his *petite amie...*"

"My wife," I said.

"You'll have to be properly married first..."

"We are." I said.

Mum smiled indulgently. She wouldn't contradict me no matter how
much she disagreed with me.

"We'll have to hear what Sibylla says about that," as usual referring it to
the oracle.

How did that fit with the fact that I was now the boss in Dad's place,
with Pepe and his workforce of straw-hatted Mexicans, and a team of
bio-chemists under Schletti. But I didn't use that as an argument to assert
my authority in opposition to the Mothers and we sat down to the fine
spread that was laid out for us: salads, charcuterie, tiny squid, artichokes
stuffed with fois gras, a variety of dishes prettily put together to tempt
jaded appetites.

"Quaintly French," said Swissified Augusta.

"Where are you staying?" Mum asked her.

"Here," I answered for her.

After that there was something charmingly polite about the evening in
which I switched roles, from son to husband. It was as if Goosie and I were
on a family visit to Mum, and when it had lasted long enough I tactfully
escorted Mum into her half of our suite and firmly closed the door between
us. Then Goosie and I sat on the balcony under the midnight blue sky while
the tables with the remains of our supper were wheeled away and the bed in
the inner room turned down and the pillows plumped up.

Our second wedding night, this time on neutral territory.

"Where do you want to live?" I asked straight off, that being where our first attempt had foundered.

"With you," she said.

"Then it will be mostly in London. That's where my home and office is, certainly until I'm finished with LSE, which it seems will drag on indefinitely. I am being called upon to lead discussions on the morality of money — as if it had any, look at my Dad, an arms dealer who lectured on ethics — and eventually it may become employment for me as part-time lecturer at the School."

"And part-time what else?"

"We'll take a flat in Basel next door to the Heini's, that's where the money is. What about you? We'd better settle it now before it's too late."

"You mean before we go to bed."

"Before you break my heart completely. I want to go on living."

"May warned me it's fairly fragile at the moment. My big sister seems well acquainted with it."

"May is not my lover. We get together occasionally when our twitchy bits become unbearably frustrated. When I have you that won't happen."

"May won't be able to get another boyfriend to fuck her, that evil troll Grimsi won't let her."

"I'm your evil troll, I won't let you have anyone else either," I said.

Goosie laughed at me.

"You're a sweetheart, Con, you'll never make a good troll. Look at you, smiley face, sexy voice, the Geneva politessinesses you put into your irresistible cock-action... how could I ever want anyone but you?"

I must have some fatal flaw, I thought. It's not possible to be worthy of this much love.

The Sibyl, custodian of the Guarneri, asked the Goose come to play on it whenever Felix Leo was at home for the holidays so that sister and brother could make music together. As a result, at regular intervals I had to fit weekends under the Virtues into my overloaded schedule. However, I discovered the rewards were well worth it. I developed a good ear for the sound of their instruments, and so, for instruments in general.

Every so often when Mrs Hein and I met for chocolate at Läderach so I could be a dutiful step-son, we would go on to drop in on Mr Mug. Mami Hein liked to see what was going in the way of art though she never bought any, while I inspected his latest musical acquisitions.

When we ran into May amongst the antique weapons, she didn't waste time in polite greetings though she let herself be Swiss-kissed on the cheeks by Roger's Mami.

"I know you're concealing something from me," she said, suspecting I had found the Sturmgewehr. She knew nothing about Dad's other two pair but she had the Sibyl's gift of guessing, just as I had Dad's.

"You've nothing to complain about," said Mami Hein. "Roger got Heini's old gun for you. Your Daddy used it in competitions, he preferred it to his own standard issue. Heini's is one of the original war-time models, Smiley liked the weight of it."

"Con is greedy and selfish," May went on grumbling, quite without justification. I refused to be drawn into a discussion about guns, and leaving the rival females to fight it out, bought a pair of early Bavarian violins I was sure Augusta would like for their sweetly melodious quality.

Apart from her sessions with Felix, Goosie had now a few talented pupils who came to the house for lessons and she had a group of them rehearsing together. Mum liked having her there and let them use the drawing-room for its great acoustics. Mum regretted now that the Steinway was gone but the Sibyl wasn't going to let us have it back. She said she needed it for inspiration.

"We could have given little concerts," Mum said. "I used to have *soirées* when we had it here in the drawing-room — not that your father liked people playing on his grandmother's old piano — it's a pity none of you inherited his talent."

Not Augusta!

It was a great relief to me that my Augusta was the one person in our extended family on whose life my Dad had had practically no impact. She must have been there as a small child when he was with the Sibyl, but I knew how she could be in the same room as May and me yet live in her own little world that had nothing to do with us. That lack of incestuous closeness was the important difference in my sentiment for the sisters. She kept that mysterious otherness I adored.

May and I had fought for our father's attention as we still fought for possession of his soul and his legacy. It was fortunate he had so much to leave, just as in life he had so much love to give. There was enough to go around. It was his grandmother's love for him that he associated with her piano, so I could well imagine him not being too keen on Mum's lady friends tinkling away on her precious Steinway at their *soirées*. I could see how he'd raise a disapproving eyebrow, but for Mum's sake he would suffer in silence. Anyone else would have heard his opinion expressed in such colourful language it left no doubt how much he disapproved.

Bhüatiströüli!

Why couldn't I find him?

I had to stop myself from going back to la Plata for another look. Only the thought of meeting Mirta's expectations kept me away from that infinite, featureless stretch of sandy dune. What had once been a truly enlightening experience would now be an embarrassment.

I sat with the Divine Sibyl watching and listening to Augusta and Felix playing a slow sad movement from Ravel's concerto for violin and violoncello, May doing the deeper part on the Guarneri, Felix Leo lifting the mood on the sharper Mittenwald.

Felix's wavy locks were such a give-away. Without that, would anyone suppose he wasn't Uncle Gus's second son? But it wasn't just the red. The hatter at Hermès recognised me by the shape of my skull even without the colour.

At nearly 15 Felix had the Sibyl's pure unblemished skin with only the lightest dusting of golden freckles, a truly beautiful boy. Grandfather used to paint pictures of the Divine Sibyl and little May, but now whenever he wasn't working on a money-making commission he almost compulsively painted Felix, from little sketches slowly growing into larger portraits. When I made some comment on the latest quite formal one he explained:

"Felix is the son I'd have liked to have. The Sibyl's son, not my wife's."

The music seemed to go on remorselessly in one somewhat discordant key and I lost concentration. Musing on Grandfather's words, I realised that until now it had never occurred to me that even he had been one of the Sibyl's devoted lovers. I wondered what the story would be if the Sibyl came down to earth and gave the one true account of her own life. But as likely as not she'd prove to be as much a shape-shifter as my trickster Dad. Was there ever one carved in stone truth?

I put out my hand to touch hers.

"I've always been in love with you," I said.

"You were such a funny, sweet child," she said, smiling at me with such tender love I had to remind myself of Mrs Hein abandoned on the edge of the abyss in the arms of Hercule — Dad's revenge. No need to do his bidding with the Sibyl. Their mutual grand passion was beyond me though I could see it and feel it.

"You have your own *aidos*. It's time for you to leave him behind," she said.

"Tell me, Sibylla, what you see happening."

"I see him swimming with dolphins," she said. "Usually they nudge him back to the shore, they won't let him stay at sea with them, they say he must endure the human condition, for good or evil, where he belongs, on land. But that day they come for him and swim around in circles to protect him from the gunmen until he drifts with them far out into the ice-cold water of the South Atlantic, too far. He is happy to go that way."

I think, it could have happened like that. It would account for why there was no body, why they found only trousers, a watch and passport. But if he were already dead with a bullet in his head? Maybe... was Mirta herself telling the truth? It occurred to me that the pistol Mirta kept hidden under her pillow could well be Dad's lost Nagant.

Give up! Let it be!

Veritas on the Sibyl's villa wall had a slyly ambiguous look, rather like the Sibyl herself...

Uncle Gus came out of his Archive to hear the music. He was a man I had great respect for. As Uncle Paul's School friend he had been a lifelong 'uncle.' Now I was no longer a child it was up to me to form a proper friendship with him, man to man.

"Will you come with me to the River Plate?" I asked him. I wasn't expecting him to say yes, but I wanted to see his reaction to my request.

"I'd be no use to you there. It's not my part of the world," he said. "Toby should have gone as soon as Sibylla asked him to. He had an acute crisis of conscience over it and it has troubled him ever since. As lawyer and friend he had an obligation to act on our suspicions but he used his Quaker scruples to stay out of any unpleasantness."

I had always considered Toby very active in Dad's interests but apparently his brother-in-law Gus had a different opinion.

"— just as he would never admit that he was involved when their friend Joey was killed. They were seventeen years old, playing Russian Roulette with the Nagant 1895 your great-grandfather brought into exile from the Tzar's army. It wasn't meant as a game or gamble but an experiment with the laws of Chance, what your father was developing as his Chaos Theory. As referee Toby should have stopped it when Joey dropped the gun but he failed to pick it up, so your father did...

Maybe it was Joey who shot him — or his *avatar* — releasing his spirit after all these years of chasing death up mountains, flying solo across continents, sailing into the still heart of storms. Dad never explained why. When he didn't want to explain something he would give the silliest possible answer and make it sound quite reasonable, but it explained Dad's reckless defiance of death, gambling his life away until it got him in the end.

I pictured myself walking that strand again trying to think what it was like for him stepping out of the waves and facing the probability that as he walked a gunman was waiting to follow on behind him. But I couldn't possibly feel it, I had never played Russian Roulette with a friend like Joey.

Mirta said he was smiling in death. Relieved at last of the burden of remorse he had carried with him since that chance bullet.

I the trousers, Roger the watch, May the passport.
We three...

www.ingramcontent.com/pod-product-compliance
Lightning Source LLC
Chambersburg PA
CBHW061253170626
46809CB00007B/2982